"I KNOW I SHOULDN'T KISS YOU, BUT I CAN'T HELP MYSELF," ROLFE MURMURED.

"You wanted to before and didn't," Milly reminded him gently.

"I seem to have lost my self-control since then," he admitted, bending his head to kiss her.

Milly quivered under his touch. When the kiss ended, they were both shaken by the ferocity of their emotions.

"Fortunately we're in the middle of a vineyard, or I might be tempted to do something we'd both regret," Rolfe said, straining for lightness.

Milly broke free from him and glared. Why did he always play it safe? Why couldn't he just let his passion overrule his reason? "For once in your life it wouldn't hurt you to do something impulsive!" she snapped.

"Do you want impulsiveness, Milly, or a man who is constant, faithful? Because if it's impulsiveness you want, then that's all you'll get."

Be sure to read this month's
CANDLELIGHT ECSTASY CLASSIC ROMANCES

NOT FOR ANY PRICE

Suzannah Davis

A CANDLELIGHT ECSTASY ROMANCE®

Published by
Dell Publishing Co., Inc.
1 Dag Hammarskjold Plaza
New York, New York 10017

For Gordon and Lynn, for the love and encouragement; and for
Mary and Devoyal, for making the trip.

Special thanks to Mr. Paul Post, Post Familie Winery, Altus,
Arkansas.

ISBN: 0-440-16454-0

Printed in the United States of America

October 1986

10 9 8 7 6 5 4 3 2 1

WFH

To Our Readers:

We have been delighted with your enthusiastic response to Candlelight Ecstasy Romances®, and we thank you for the interest you have shown in this exciting series.

In the upcoming months we will continue to present the distinctive sensuous love stories you have come to expect only from Ecstasy. We look forward to bringing you many more books from your favorite authors and also the very finest work from new authors of contemporary romantic fiction.

As always, we are striving to present the unique, absorbing love stories that you enjoy most—books that are more than ordinary romance. Your suggestions and comments are always welcome. Please write to us at the address below.

Sincerely,

The Editors
Candlelight Romances
1 Dag Hammarskjold Plaza
New York, New York 10017

CHAPTER ONE

"Stop that man!"

The disturbing command interrupted Millicent Carter's singsong auctioneer's chant and sent invisible shock waves through the seated audience. Milly pointed an accusing finger at the retreating back of the tall blond man leaving the exclusive auction gallery.

"Frank, stop him!" she shouted to the elderly security guard. Frank, grizzled and stooped in his blue uniform, shuffled after the suspect, the butt of his pistol shaking in time with the stainless steel handcuffs on his belt.

"What is it, Milly?" demanded Gerald Anderson, the proprietor of Hot Spring's Park Place Gallery.

"He's got that woman's ring!" Milly exclaimed, shoving the auctioneer's gavel into the startled hands of her corpulent employer. She raced down the aisle between the rows of red velvet-covered chairs, darted through the entrance, then skidded to a halt on the broad sidewalk. The evening throng of tourists in town for the famous Hot Springs baths and the horseracing season filled the expanse of pavement, temporarily blocking her view. Then she saw the top of a blond head rising above the bobbing crowd, and her gray-green eyes darkened with anger.

"He won't get away with this!" she muttered fiercely, charging down the sidewalk after the culprit in her best imitation of a superhero. She dodged around sauntering couples and small children with dripping ice cream cones. She threaded her way past elderly tourists in bright summer sportswear. Just ahead she spotted a panting Frank trotting gamely after the thief, and Milly hastened after them both, her movements swift and sure.

She knew all along he was up to no good, she told herself as she ran. She had been aware of the man all during the evening's auction as he sat silently in the last row. The display of dozens of crystal chandeliers that hung in the gallery had illuminated his fair hair and rather austere good looks. Now, she thought grimly, she would be able to pick him out of a lineup! From her position at the podium she had seen him reach into the empty seat beside him and relieve another customer of a small paper bag that bore the auction house's distinctive logo. The nerve! To attempt such a thing in full view! Mr. Anderson had given her lecture after lecture about security in the gallery, but to actually catch a thief as slick as this one would be the thrill of a lifetime.

Milly redoubled her efforts and passed Frank, who was now gasping for breath, his face purple.

"Come on!" she panted, ignoring the curious glances they received. Luckily their quarry did not seem to be aware of their pursuit. Milly had to give him credit; he certainly was a cool one.

"Hey, you! Stop!" she shouted. Many heads turned, but the blond man did not slow down, did not even look back. The sudden fear that he would escape sent Milly plunging after him, her feet pounding down the pavement. The rhythmic patter must have alerted the man just as Milly bore down on him, for he turned an instant before she careened wildly into him, his handsome face a comical study of shock and sudden horror.

Milly hit the man squarely in his chest with her shoulder and they both fell to the sidewalk under the force of her onslaught. They tumbled into the outdoor display of a nearby gift shop and sent dozens of empty white plastic water jugs flying into the street.

Strong hands clasped Milly's waist as they rolled, sparing her the brunt of the fall, but her hands and knees scraped painfully on the rough cement. Milly felt the breath go out of her prey with a loud whoosh as they came to an abrupt halt against the brick facade of a building. Plastic jugs bounced noisily in all directions. Milly let go a triumphant cry as she straddled the man's chest, effectively pinning him to the pavement.

"Ah-ha! Got you!" she crowed, her thick brunette hair spilling into her flushed face. Her hands and knees were scraped, her nylons were in tatters and her jersey dress was hiked up too high on her shapely thighs to be modest. Blithely ignoring all this, she grabbed the lapels of the man's conservative brown suit and bounced triumphantly on his chest. A tortured gasp escaped his lips.

An excited murmur of astonishment passed through the crowd that gathered. Milly looked up as Frank pushed through the tangle of bodies.

"Frank, quick!" she cried. "Get your handcuffs on him before he gets his breath!" Frank's jaw hung open in stupefaction at the picture of a green-eyed beauty astride a prostrate giant. The giant in question groaned as he sucked air painfully back into empty lungs. "Frank!" Milly hollered as her precarious seating rocked with the man's indrawn breath.

Frank hurriedly unhooked his handcuffs from his heavy belt, but his hands were shaking so badly he

9

could not fasten them around the culprit's wrist without Milly's assistance. Unfortunately, due to the man's position, it was impossible to attach the other cuff behind his back, so Milly did the next best thing—she locked her own wrist into the pair of cuffs.

"Now try to get away," she chortled, shaking her hand and rattling the chains.

"For God's sake, woman, .get off!" the thief demanded. His hands slid up the smooth flesh of her thighs and lingered for an instant. Then he twisted beneath Milly and gave her a push, sliding her off onto her rump. But even this indignity could not dampen her elation.

"Call the police, Frank," she instructed, grinning at the older man.

The thief groaned, rolling onto his side. Milly lurched as he took her with him. "What the hell?" he muttered, opening dazed eyes the color of an Arkansas summer sky.

"Just relax, mister," Milly advised, her grin getting even wider. "You aren't going anywhere."

With an abrupt movement the man sat up, shaking his head to clear it. He raised his hand to smooth back the shock of yellow hair that had fallen forward on his brow, but the handcuffs linked to Milly's wrist stopped the motion in mid-flight. He glared at the handcuffs, then at Milly's smug expression, and then at the crowd around them. A flush of color rose under his tanned cheeks, and his square jaw tightened.

"Young woman," he said grimly from between clenched teeth, "what's the meaning of this?"

"As if you don't know," Milly scoffed. "You can tell your story to the police in a minute, but don't waste your breath on me. *I* saw it all!"

"Police?" His thick brows drew together in a perplexed frown. Milly's respect for his acting ability increased. To take a con artist like this off the streets would indeed be a public service, she decided. Just then Gerald Anderson pushed through the mob.

"Good God!" he roared. "What have you done, Milly?"

Now it was Milly's turn to look puzzled. "Done? Why, I caught this thief!"

"He's no thief!" Anderson bellowed. Beads of sweat trickled down his jowls and dripped into the collar of his Western-style leisure suit. He ran a finger around his tight neckline, touching the solid gold diamond-studded collar points as if for reassurance. "Mr. Hart, sir! Are you all right?"

"What do you mean, he's no thief?" Milly demanded, staring up at her infuriated boss. "I saw him take it! It's got to be around here someplace." She looked in vain for the small white bag that held the loot. "All right, what did you do with it?" she snapped at the man beside her.

"Do with what?" Rolfe Hart returned suspiciously.

"Don't give me that!" Milly muttered. Before he had a chance to react, she frisked him, reaching inside his suit coat to check his pockets and running her free hand across the hard expanse of his chest beneath his crisp white shirt.

"Stop that!" Rolfe growled, grabbing her wrist. Their eyes met for a breathless instant, and Milly felt a frisson of mutual awareness sear her nerves. The crowd tittered, and he dropped her wrist as if burned.

"It's got to be here," Milly repeated, a bit shaken. Suddenly her expression cleared as she realized she was sitting on a much-abused paper bag. She pulled it free, then waved it under Mr. Anderson's quivering chin. "Just look in there!" she ordered.

Anderson snatched the proffered package from her hand, wrenched it open and removed a small blue velvet jewel box. The bystanders moaned on a collective sigh when he opened the box to reveal the glittering diamond-and-sapphire dinner ring. Anderson's eyes bulged, and Milly could see the veins in his temple throb.

"Ms. Carter—you're fired!" Anderson screeched. Around them, the crowd murmured in amazement.

"Wha—what?" Milly was dumbfounded. Her full lips shaped an O, and her eyes widened as she glanced first at the man still seated on the pavement beside her, then at her furious ex-employer.

"It never occurred to you that Mr. Hart had a perfect right to take that ring, did it?" Anderson asked sarcastically. "If you had been on duty on time for once, you might have been aware that he had made arrangements to pick up his mother's ring earlier." Then he turned his attention to Rolfe Hart directly. "I'm sorry about all this, sir."

"His mother's!" Milly shrilled as a sickening feeling galloped along her nerve ends and landed with a vengeance in the pit of her stomach. A small, horrified whimper escaped her lips. "Oh, no, I've done it again!" She sent a cringing look at Rolfe Hart's stern expression, then hastily glanced away, shuddering. Well, she'd really done it this time. Better see if she could salvage the situation.

"Mr. Anderson, let me explain," she began weakly. She struggled to her feet, and of necessity, Rolfe followed her, placing a steadying hand on her elbow when she staggered, slightly off balance. Milly gulped but refused to look at him again. "You see, he picked up the bag, and there was a woman next to him, and you'd told me over and over again to be wary of rip-off artists and—"

"Enough! I don't want to hear any of your far-fetched explanations!" Mr. Anderson exploded. "I'll see that you never work in Hot Springs again after what you've done tonight. Just get out of my sight! If I ever see you again it'll be too soon!" Milly's shoulders slumped. She bit her lip and studied her shoes as she struggled to control her dismay. It would be too humiliating to break down and cry in front of all these people.

Anderson was speaking to Rolfe Hart again. "Please accept my apologies. Come back to the gallery for coffee and you can clean up a bit." Rolfe dusted the clinging dirt and debris from his once immaculate suit, then lifted a sardonic eyebrow.

"No need," he said curtly. "There's no real harm done. But I'd be obliged if you could do something about this." He lifted his hand to display his and Milly's shackled wrists. "If you'll remove these cuffs, we'll forget about the whole thing."

"Oh, thank you. I'm terribly sorry. I'll have your suit cleaned," Milly babbled. She attempted to add her efforts to brush off his suit, but Rolfe flinched with such distaste that she dropped her hand dejectedly.

"Good God!" Mr. Anderson groaned. "Frank, do something, will you?"

The elderly guard shuffled forward with the most awful look on his face that Milly had ever seen. He wrung his hands and seemed almost in tears.

"Mr. Anderson, sir. You know I've been working for the gallery nigh on to thirty years now. Went to work for your father, I did," Frank croaked.

"Yes, yes! Never mind all that now," Mr. Anderson interrupted. "Just get the key and release Mr. Hart!"

"That's what I'm trying to tell you, sir," Frank whimpered miserably. "I can't!"

"What!" Three voices joined in a unison of dismay.

"I lost that there key some twenty-nine years ago,"

13

Frank moaned, shaking his head. "Never needed it 'fore now . . ."

Slowly Rolfe and Milly turned toward each other, their expressions aghast. It was hard to decide who was more horrified: Rolfe, tied to a woman of unpredictable disposition bent on his public humiliation; or Milly, linked to a man whose wrath she knew she undoubtedly deserved!

Twenty minutes later, after the most awkward silence she had ever endured, Milly stole a covert glance at Rolfe Hart. Her heart sank at the unrelenting annoyance she saw in his expression, and she sighed.

"Will you please refrain from that infernal sighing!" Rolfe demanded, making Milly jump in her uncomfortable straightbacked chair.

"Sorry," she muttered, glancing anywhere but at him. They had been whisked back to the Park Place Gallery and deposited like so much excess baggage in a back office. Mr. Anderson was in another office trying to locate a locksmith, so far without any success. Milly hated to contemplate how much longer she would be tied to Rolfe Hart.

They sat close together, their imprisoned wrists resting on their thighs. Without actually studying him openly, she knew that he was probably in his midthirties, stood a little over six feet tall, and was lean and strongly muscled beneath his well-tailored suit. Milly slowly became aware of the warmth that radiated from his powerful body. Rolfe raised a tan hand and ran a lean finger under his starched shirt collar. Small golden hairs curled from under his cuff, and his hand was callused from outdoor work, which surprised Milly a bit. His urbane, square-jawed exterior suggested that he might be a busy executive, and she wondered at the incongruity.

Milly shifted in her chair. The scrapes on her palms and knees stung unmercifully. She wished she could wash up and comb her hair, and her patience, never her strong suit, was being tried to the limit by the taciturn man beside her.

"Must you wriggle so?" Rolfe questioned sourly, and Milly's temper flared.

"Well, I'm sorry!" she sputtered. "But I'm not used to being attached to another person like some kind of —of overgrown parasite!"

"And you suppose I am?" he returned, his deep voice dripping with sarcasm.

"No, of course not." Milly sighed. "I'm sor—"

"For God's sake, don't apologize again!" he snapped.

"Why not?" she replied mournfully. "I'm very good at it. Things like this happen to me all the time."

"Then God help us all, Miss—what *is* your name?" he demanded. Milly looked up into his blue eyes and suddenly realized how gorgeous they were. Wide set, and fringed by thick sandy lashes, they were a rich, clear blue.

"It's Milly, er, Millicent Carter," she said, bringing her thoughts to earth with some difficulty.

"Well, Milly Carter, if things like this happen all the time, your life must be a walking disaster!" he said, showing his irritation. Milly's lower lip suddenly trembled, and she looked away, blinking.

"I suppose you've got enough reason to feel that way," she replied in a low voice.

Rolfe moved uncomfortably. He hadn't meant to hurt her feelings, he thought crossly. But *disaster* was the only word he could think of when dealing with most women, and this loony woman in particular. But she needn't look at him like a kitten that had just been kicked, either. His rising feelings of sympathy were instantly quashed as Milly squared her small shoulders and made a preposterous announcement.

"It's not all my fault, anyway," she said. "If you hadn't been sitting back there all evening looking just as though you were sizing up the joint, this never would have happened."

"What! How can you say that?"

"You didn't bid a single time," Milly argued. "That in itself is suspicious. Face it, you looked like a slick character with evil intentions."

Rolfe jerked upright in his seat. "That's absurd!" he denied with injured dignity. "It's obvious you have an overactive imagination, young lady!" Milly gave him a wide-eyed look, then inspected him from his stylish haircut down his muscular length to the tips of his polished shoes. She acknowledged to herself that Rolfe Hart was a very attractive man.

"All right, I'll admit you don't look like a hardened jewel thief," she said as she studied him, the tip of a finger absently tracing the stitching of his lapel. Then she gave a little laugh, and her mouth curved upward, filling her face with a beguiling innocence that belied her twenty-six years. "I give up. What do you do for a living?"

"Here, take this," Rolfe instructed gruffly, pushing a spotless white handkerchief into her hand. "I'd prefer that you not bleed all over the suit. It's taken enough punishment today already."

"Oh, sorry." Milly accepted the linen and began dabbing at the grazed places on her palm.

"And to answer your question, I'm a viniculturist."

"A who?" Milly's expression was suddenly alive with interest.

Rolfe was dazed by the brilliance of her incredible gray-green gaze, accentuated by finely arched brows and thick dark lashes. He cleared his throat.

16

"My family has vineyards and a winery," he said.

"In Arkansas?" Milly asked skeptically.

"Certainly. The northwest portion of the state is a quality grape producing region."

"The only thing I know about grapes is that they come from the grocery store," Milly said. Her self-deprecating laugh was charming enough to soften even the hardest heart.

Rolfe blinked, momentarily taken aback by her artless admission. He was fast coming to realize that Milly Carter was a very unusual woman. Not that he hadn't noticed that when she mowed him down like so much hay.

He could still feel the impact of her slight form against his more massive bulk, and his palms tingled as he remembered the shape of her slim curves. Milly lifted her luxurious brown mane from her neck for coolness. Rolfe watched the innate grace of her movements with growing fascination, then wondered fleetingly what it would be like to push back that thick fall of hair and test the skin at the nape of her sweet neck. He swallowed, bringing his wayward thoughts back under control.

"We do grow a table variety, but most of our grapes are processed into wine. Do you find it warm in here?" he asked suddenly. He tugged at the tie knotted at his throat and unbuttoned his collar.

"It is a bit close, now that you mention it. Here, let me help you off with your jacket," Milly offered. Suddenly she began to giggle. "I think there's a small problem here."

"Oh, I see." Rolfe realized that although he could take his jacket off, it would have to stop at his handcuffed wrist. "That's all right, then."

"No, go ahead," Milly insisted, reaching around with her free left hand to ease the jacket from his shoulders. She helped Rolfe shrug out of the jacket, pulling it down his captured arm until it bunched up around their joined hands. "Now, that's better, isn't it?" She smiled ingenuously.

Rolfe was not so sure. The touch of her hand across his back had been rather disconcerting.

"You know," Milly continued conversationally as she settled back down in her chair, "I'm really amazed at myself."

"Is that so?" Rolfe frowned slightly.

"I still don't know how I managed to knock you down," she said, admiring the width of his shoulders. "I'm a featherweight compared to you."

"You had the element of surprise on your side," Rolfe replied dryly.

"I certainly did! You should have seen your face!" Milly laughed.

Rolfe's lips twitched. "Miss Carter—"

"Oh, call me Milly." She laughed again. "It would be silly not to now that our relationship is so, er— intimate."

Rolfe raised his eyes. "Are you always quite so irrepressible?"

"I'm afraid so," she replied cheerfully.

"Then you must drive the people around you to distraction," he grumbled.

"Not always." She grinned. "I just know how to make the best of a bad situation."

"And is this a bad situation?" Rolfe asked.

Milly glanced around, then answered in a conspiratorial whisper. "Believe it or not, this isn't so bad. Only rates a five or six on the old disaster meter."

"I would have thought losing your job would rate a ten," Rolfe pointed out with maddening logic.

Milly was suddenly pensive. "Yes, well, there is that . . ." She trailed off as she dabbed at her scratched

18

knees with his handkerchief, pulling gingerly at her ruined stockings.

It was quite a blow to one's ego to be summarily dismissed from one's position, Milly thought, especially when one thought she was rendering a service above and beyond the call of duty. Unconsciously she sighed again as the silence between them lengthened. She supposed she'd have to consider seriously the inquiry she'd received from that historical society. It wasn't a matter of money, as her accountant could testify, but Milly needed to feel useful, and doing the job she was trained for was the best way she knew.

Rolfe's eyes narrowed slightly as Milly carefully worked on her injured knees. Milly's abrupt silence was making him feel uncomfortable again.

"Ah—I suppose that if you look at this one way," he ventured, "you would be considered a heroine. After all, it was a fairly courageous thing to do, running me down. What if I had been a real jewel thief?"

Milly glanced up in surprise. "Why, thank you, Rolfe. That's very generous of you."

"In fact, firing you is much too drastic a solution, in my opinion," he continued, warming to the subject.

Milly smiled and shrugged. "Oh, well, things weren't working out here anyway. I'm not overly fond of tacky Italian porcelain," she said, referring to the ornate and gaudy pieces that crowded every inch of the gallery. "I really prefer to deal with antiques and artwork and Americana."

"Oh? How did you get interested in that?" he asked.

"I have my degree in fine arts with emphasis on period furniture," she explained, surprising him. "That's what I really enjoy. It seemed natural to get an auctioneer's license so I could deal with a vast array of fine antiques. This is my first gallery job. I normally work free-lance."

"You're not from here?"

"No. I'm from Little Rock, but I move from job to job as they come up. Auctioneering is a pretty uncertain life."

"I can imagine," Rolfe said dryly.

Milly returned her attention to her knees. She was unconscious of the fact that Rolfe's eyes moved admiringly over the shapely turn of her ankles, calves and a goodly portion of her slim thighs, where her skirt had been turned back.

"I wonder what's taking them so long," he said hoarsely.

Milly glanced up to find his eyes focused on her legs. She blushed, then dropped her skirt into place and handed his handkerchief back to him.

"I suppose locksmiths are hard to come by this late in the evening," she said. "We could probably get the police to remove them. In fact, if I had a hammer I could get them off right now!"

"Oh, no, you wouldn't!" Rolfe protested, visions of a hammer-wielding Milly Carter filling his mind. "I just wish they'd hurry. I could use a drink."

"Do you think that would be wise, considering the, er, delicacy of our situation?" Milly asked mischievously. A bubbling laugh escaped her.

A curious set of expressions flickered across Rolfe's face; then he frowned fiercely. "Will you stop giggling? I fail to see any humor in our present circumstances!"

Milly struggled to control her twitching lips. "No, you're right," she said, forcing a serious expression onto her face, but her eyes continued to dance. "This isn't funny, except . . ."

Rolfe shook his head in total befuddlement. He had the feeling he was fast losing control, and the sensation was an unaccustomed and uncomfortable one.

"Except what?" he demanded.

"You aren't married, are you?" she asked.

"What?" Rolfe had trouble following this abrupt change of subject. "No, I'm not. Why?"

"Well, what if they can't get us loose? We'd be linked for life! It couldn't be any worse if we were married!"

"Miss Carter," Rolfe said in his iciest voice, "I can't think of anyone I'd want to marry less than you! What a nightmare for the man unlucky enough to find himself in such a situation!"

Milly's mouth dropped open at this attack. Then her eyes lit with the fire of battle. "Well, that goes double for me, *Mr.* Hart!" she said huffily. Her chin shot up at a belligerent angle. "You obviously have no sense of humor! Who'd want to marry a stuffed shirt like you, anyway?"

Rolfe's strangled cry of outraged irritation was smothered as Mr. Anderson, Frank, and a man in green coveralls burst into the room.

"All right, Mr. Hart," Anderson said heartily. "Here we are! Sam will have you out of those cuffs in a jiffy!" He hovered over the operation as Sam the locksmith tried a series of skeleton keys.

"Them's top-quality handcuffs," Frank muttered on one side of the room. "Had 'em thirty years!"

"Got it!" Sam exclaimed, and Milly felt the cold metal cuffs fall away from her wrist. Her arm felt curiously weightless now that she was no longer bound to Rolfe's intimidating bulk. She rubbed her wrist where the metal had chafed her skin.

"Now, if you don't mind, Ms. Carter," Anderson boomed. "I'd like you to remove yourself from my premises immediately!"

"Of course, Mr. Anderson," Milly said resignedly, moving toward the door. She paused, glancing with some trepidation at Rolfe's stony countenance.

"I'm truly sorry for the inconvenience, Rolfe," she murmured. Her expression was contrite as she looked at Rolfe's impassive face. He had draped his suit coat over one arm and hooked a thumb into his pocket.

"That's quite all right," Rolfe replied formally.

Milly gave Rolfe a lopsided smile that quite unexpectedly tugged at his heartstrings.

" 'Bye." Her gesture of farewell was curiously childlike. Then she disappeared out the office door. Mr. Anderson began a droning monologue of renewed apologies, to which Rolfe gave only half his attention.

Rolfe watched Milly leave with mixed feelings. He could hardly contain his exasperation with this pretty, unpredictable woman, but those feelings were complicated by an undeniable physical attraction that had caught him off guard. It was a dangerous combination, certain to flare out of control at the first opportunity. He ignored the faint regret that accompanied her departure and tried to concentrate on the enormous relief he felt to be finally free of those steel fetters and Milly's insidious charm. There was no doubt in his mind that he had made a lucky escape. Thank God, he'd never have to see that crazy lady again!

CHAPTER TWO

Milly ground the gears once again, then eased her rattling candy-apple-red jeep over the slight rise and down into the sheltered valley that cradled the little town of Altus. To either side rose the slopes of the Ozark mountains, the green of their foliage misty now with a midsummer haze. She had left Hot Springs early that morning, nursing her temperamental conveyance over the gradually building inclines as she marveled at the scenic beauty of the region.

Each new vista presented another delight. The rocky mountain outcroppings boasted hardwoods and conifers resplendent in their full summer foliage. The mid-July heat barely penetrated the floor of the forests through which she had driven. There seemed a kind of hush, an almost reverent silence, that hung over the country, as if merely biding its time until the more colorful autumn season. As she neared her destination, the land began to flatten, and Milly found herself in lush countryside.

It was lucky happenstance that the Altus Historical Society had decided to sponsor an auction just when Milly found herself out of a job. Correspondence with the secretary of the society, a Miss Abington, had been very cordial. The society wished to sponsor an antiques auction of some magnitude—large enough to draw interested buyers from several counties and perhaps as far away as Fort Smith and Little Rock. They needed an expert to organize the sale, write the catalog, and see to publicity for the event, to be held in about six weeks in conjunction with the annual Grape Festival. Since her lodgings would be provided, Milly had not minded that the fee they were offering was fairly low. At least it would be a change from the Park Place Gallery, and heaven knew she could do with a change after that fiasco two weeks ago!

She smiled as she caught a glimpse of a geometrically terraced vineyard on a distant hillside and realized that she had reached the wine-producing country of Arkansas. It really was too bad she wasn't likely ever to run into Rolfe Hart again. He had been just about the sexiest winemaker Milly had ever met—not that she'd met very many. And too bad he had such a sour disposition, for a genuine smile on that handsome face would have been really something!

The jeep gave a strangled cough and jerked convulsively as Milly shifted gears to slow her descent into the sleepy little town. A few cars passed her as she turned onto the main street, and several pedestrians paused to gaze in amazement at her rattling, wheezing progress. Milly waved cheerfully, blithely unconcerned, then turned off the main highway. Her dark shining hair was confined at her nape with a flowing scarf the same cheery red as her jeep, and her eyes were concealed behind oversize sunglasses. She wore jeans for comfort and a colorful cotton blouse for coolness, air-conditioning being an amenity unknown to jeeps.

Milly craned her neck to study the hand-drawn map on the seat beside her. She was to join the Saturday-afternoon meeting of the Altus Historical Society, but it was difficult to follow someone else's directions, especially when "house on the right" might describe sev-

24

eral of the modest homes in this shady neighborhood! She braked, slowing her progress to study the street, but could see no house number or other indication of her destination. She would have to ask someone.

She topped a small hill, coming up behind a perspiring jogger. Perhaps he could help her. It was obvious that he was fighting the battle of the middle-aged bulge—and probably losing, Milly thought humorously. His hair was thinning in the back, and he plodded along, his "spare tire" jiggling under a trendy jogging tank top and shorts. Milly was on the verge of pulling up beside him to ask directions when the man scowled back at her over his shoulder, then impatiently waved her around him. He was so obviously bad-tempered about the whole thing that Milly kept going.

As she drove on, the style of the homes reminded her of miniature versions of cousin Howard Carter's Little Rock mansion. It was merely a showplace and hardly suitable for the rearing of a rambunctious five-year-old. Not that she had actually spent much time there. Boarding school for Milly had been the answer to soothe the old man's shattered nerves, and Milly couldn't blame him for seeking that solution. Her parents' untimely deaths in a boating accident had made Howard sole guardian of the young heiress to the Carter Petroleum fortune, a role hardly suited to his solitary inclinations and bachelor's life-style. Still, Cousin Howard had done his best, educating her, if not loving her, until his death six years earlier, and if Milly had been a disappointment to him in her refusal to enter Little Rock society, then he had to be satisfied that she was a dutiful ward and that her minor scrapes had never really inconvenienced him.

It had always seemed to Milly that her money surrounded her with a glittering yet impenetrable barrier

25

that separated her from the outside world. Swiss finishing schools had polished her, but Milly had never been overly concerned with which fork to use or who were the "in" people in Palm Beach this year. Rather, she had hungered for real human contact, becoming fascinated with the individual differences of each person she met. When she had at last been old enough to please herself, she had chosen a life-style that played down her wealthy background and allowed her the freedom she had been denied growing up. It was one of the reasons she raced ahead full steam to meet whatever life offered. She often felt she had to make up for lost time, and if sometimes her impetuosity got her into hot water, then it was a price she paid willingly for the experience.

She gave a sigh of relief a minute later when she spotted a man mowing his lawn a bit further down the street. She pulled the jeep to the edge of the narrow street, switched off the ignition, removed her sunglasses, then climbed out just as the man turned the corner between two identical driveways.

"Hi!" she yelled over the noise of the lawnmower. "Can you help me? I think I'm lost!" The man looked up, indicated with a grin that he couldn't hear her, and bent to turn off the mower. He was tall and lanky, with dark hair and kind eyes, and was dressed in well-worn shorts and T-shirt. He walked toward her, mopping his brow, as the mower thudded into silence.

"What was that again?" he asked, friendliness radiating from his long face.

"I said—"

"Damn mutt!"

Milly turned at these harshly uttered words just as a ferocious yipping broke out. The jogger she had passed earlier had come up behind them. From the bushes a ragged puppy alternately attacked and retreated, barking fiercely at the jogger's flapping shoelaces. The man kicked out at the pup.

"Hey, don't do that!" Milly protested. She reached out and scooped the dog out of harm's reach.

"He lies in wait, just looking for a chance to sink his teeth into me!" the runner panted. He was of medium stature, somewhere over forty, and had pale, cold eyes. Milly took an instant dislike to him.

"This little fellow couldn't hurt a flea!" she defended. "Whose puppy is it?"

"It must be a stray." The lanky man had come up behind Milly and offered this explanation. "I think he likes you, Dean," he said, grinning.

"Mind your own business, Ben," Dean growled. "Give him here. He's a nuisance. I'll see that he's destroyed properly."

"You most certainly will not!" Milly snapped. "Not if I have anything to say about it!"

"Who the hell are you, anyway?" Dean demanded, wiping his brow with his matching terry wristbands.

"My name's Milly Carter, and I'm not going to let you abuse this poor, defenseless animal!"

"Suit yourself, lady. But if I ever see that mangy mutt again, that'll be the end of him!" Dean warned darkly. Turning, he jogged off down the street.

Milly barely resisted an urge to stick her tongue out at his retreating back. The puppy squirmed contentedly in Milly's arms, drawing her attention back to her new charge.

"Isn't he a sweet thing?" she crooned, entranced by the dog's floppy ears and oversize paws.

"Who, Dean Singleton?" the man called Ben teased, hands on hips. "No way! Pompous a—opps! Sorry!"

"My sentiments exactly," Milly agreed. "A thoroughly unpleasant man. Thanks for your help. I'm

Milly Carter." She offered her hand, and Ben shook it firmly, his long face split by a wide grin.

"Pleased to meet you, Milly. I'm Ben Rollins. What can I do for you?"

"I'm lost, I think," Milly explained with a smile. "Do you happen to know where the Altus Historical Society is meeting today?"

"No problem," Ben said. "It's right next door."

"Great!"

The friendly toot-toot of a horn sounded on the street behind Milly. Ben raised a hand in an easy salute, and Milly turned, adding her own wave and sending a sunny smile toward the passerby. It was a shock to suddenly recognize the driver of the blue pickup truck, but Milly would have known that handsome face anywhere.

Rolfe Hart's astonished expression mirrored Milly's surprise, and his jaw dropped as he saw her standing on the lawn with his friend Ben. For an instant Rolfe was too stunned to react; then he stepped on the brake hard. But it was too late. His rubbernecking had shifted his attention at just the wrong moment. Instead of turning into the driveway, the truck skidded right into the rear of Milly's jeep!

Milly's eyes widened in dismay at the tinkle of breaking glass. Ben's reaction was more forceful.

"Good God, Rolfe! What have you done?"

Milly could hear the mumble of a suppressed curse, then the vigorous slamming of a truck door. She unconsciously tightened her grip on the puppy. Rolfe Hart strode around the back of his truck, sent a baleful glare at the jeep, then rounded on Milly.

"What are *you* doing here?" he demanded.

"You hit my jeep," Milly said in amazement, ignoring his question. Her eyes were wide and green with accusation.

28

"I know damn well I did!" Rolfe roared. "I want to know what the blazes it's doing here in the first place! Are you following me?"

"What? Don't be ridiculous!"

"Say, do you two know each other?" Ben asked innocently.

"No!" said Milly.

"Yes!" said Rolfe.

"Sort of," amended Milly. She glared at Rolfe to disguise the fact that his antipathy hurt. It was understandable that he would be embarrassed that he had plowed into the back of her jeep, but did he have to make his dislike of her so obvious?

He wore khaki slacks that molded his lean thighs to perfection and a white cotton shirt with the cuffs rolled back over his muscular forearms. Milly's breath caught as the fabric of his shirt stretched tautly over his broad shoulders. Drat this infuriating man! He was even better-looking than she remembered.

"Well, that makes everything perfectly clear," Ben said humorously.

"I met Milly the last time I was in Hot Springs," Rolfe replied.

"No! She's not the one who—you're kidding!" Ben laughed, eyeing Milly's slim figure with new respect while she blushed furiously. She was absolutely enraged that Rolfe had told Ben the story of her humiliating escapade.

"Yeah, she's the one," Rolfe said. His brows drew together in a frown, and his jaw tightened. "You still haven't told me what you're doing in Altus."

"That, Mr. Hart, is none of your business," Milly replied stiffly. "Rest assured it has nothing to do with you! I certainly had no idea you lived here or I would have had second thoughts, too! Come on, Sebastian, let's see how bad it is."

She carried the dog toward the rear of the jeep, stepping gingerly over the shattered glass that lay in the street.

Ben followed her. "You've given him a name already? Does that mean you intend to keep the pup?" he asked.

"Sure, why not?" Milly replied absently. She scratched Sebastian behind the ears and tried to peer between the two vehicles. "Rolfe, will you please back this thing up so I can see what kind of damage there is?"

Rolfe blinked in speechless befuddlement, hoping for a ridiculous moment that it was all a bad dream. But it seemed this nightmare wasn't going away, so he did as she asked. When he backed the truck away, he rejoined Ben and Milly at the rear of the jeep.

"Could be worse," Milly mused, delicately picking the glass shards from a shattered taillight. Rolfe's truck had suffered nothing more than a scratch on the chrome bumper. She put Sebastian into the jeep, and he instantly began to investigate the interior in typical doggy fashion.

"I will, of course, have it repaired for you," Rolfe announced. His chagrin at having done something so stupid made him sound cold and unconcerned.

Milly glanced at him resentfully. "That won't be necessary. I'll get the light replaced at a service station or something."

"I must insist. I am entirely responsible and I won't have you traveling through the mountains in a vehicle that might be unsafe," Rolfe replied, his tone brooking no argument, but Milly ignored that.

"Oh, knock it off!" Milly said rudely. "I haven't got the time to argue with you simply because you've got a guilty conscience. I'm already late for my appointment. Ben, which house did you say?" she asked as Rolfe glowered at her.

"This one next door," Ben said. His wide mouth twitched in amusement.

"What!" Rolfe stared.

"She's looking for Amalie," Ben offered, relishing his normally placid friend's unusual lack of composure. He had never seen Rolfe so ruffled.

"No, I'm looking for the Altus Historical Society. A Miss Abington, I think," Milly said.

"No!" Rolfe groaned, his expression horrified. "You don't mean you're the one she hired!"

"I've been hired by the Altus Historical Society to run their auction," Milly said defensively. "What has that got to do with you?"

"Just about everything, unfortunately," Rolfe said with a groan. His hand cupped Milly's elbow, and her heart began to pound in double time. "Come on, we might as well get this over with. I'll take you."

"Take me where?" Milly had a sudden sinking sensation in the pit of her stomach. Rolfe scooped the puppy out of the interior of the jeep with his other hand. Sebastian made no protest but lay docilely in his arms.

"Ben, do you mind cleaning up that glass for me?" Rolfe asked.

"Sure, no problem. You two go ahead," Ben said, grinning. He was obviously enjoying the unusual situation thoroughly.

"Take me where?" Milly again demanded, but Rolfe was hurrying her up the paved driveway toward the small native stone bungalow set back from the street.

"To meet the president of the historical society," Rolfe said. He shot Milly a sideways glance, then dropped the bombshell. "She's my mother!"

Milly was too shocked by this startling information

31

to protest as Rolfe escorted her into the house. She groaned inwardly at the sly twist of fate that had again thrust her into Rolfe Hart's well-ordered life. Everything she did seemed to displease him, and she was woman enough to regret that they couldn't be friends. It was amazing how even the briefest encounter struck sparks that threatened to make her lose control. And Milly suspected that it was the fact that she could get under his skin that irritated Rolfe most. She wondered rather desperately if there was any way she could get out of this auction altogether.

Rolfe left the puppy in the kitchen, then led Milly toward the sound of voices drifting from the living room.

The scene that greeted them could have been straight out of a thirties period English movie. The room was furnished with overstuffed flowered chintz sofas and armchairs. A slender woman with threads of silver through her golden curls bent gracefully over a china tea service. She could only be Rolfe's mother. Two elderly women in hats and flowing dresses held fluted teacups on their knees, their faded brown eyes focusing with interest on Milly and Rolfe as they entered the room. Milly's face brightened with unconcealed delight at the homey warmth and comfort of the room.

"Mother, you have a guest," Rolfe said laconically. "Milly Carter, this is my mother, Amalie Hart."

"Why, Miss Carter, welcome!" Amalie said, smiling warmly as she rose to greet Milly. "The historical society is just delighted to have you! Did you have any trouble finding the house?"

"Well . . ."

"I ran into Milly outside," Rolfe explained. Milly had to force back a giggle at his choice of words, and as Rolfe realized what he had said, the tips of his ears began to redden. "If you'll excuse me, Mother, I have a couple of things to attend to. I'll rejoin you in a few minutes."

"Certainly, dear," Amalie said.

"Such a nice boy," murmured one of the other women as Rolfe left the room. Milly gave a start, then suppressed a wry grin with difficulty. Rolfe Hart, good-looking, masculine hunk, was hardly a boy, as her elevated pulse could testify!

"I'm very proud of Rolfe," Amalie replied. "He's taking off just to help me when he's so very busy! It's the middle of the grape harvest, you know," she explained as she drew Milly into the room.

"No, I don't know much about grapes," Milly admitted, enchanted with Amalie's friendly manner.

"Well, you're bound to learn a lot while you're here, then. May I call you Milly?" At Milly's nod, Amalie continued cheerfully. "I'm so glad that you could come today. We normally meet in the city hall, but an informal meeting is so much more efficient, don't you think?"

Before Milly quite knew what had happened, she was seated on the overstuffed sofa with her own delicate china cup on her knee. Amalie introduced her to the two elderly sisters, Louella and Florie Abington.

"Florie, of course, you have met through our correspondence," Amalie said. "And Louella also serves on the auction committee, although, now that you are here, we don't expect to have much to do! I'll admit we need professional help desperately. We've been stumbling around in the dark." Milly's half-formed intention of getting out of the job died an instant death. There was nothing that appealed to her more than to be needed.

"I'm really looking forward to it," Milly said.

"It's a new project for the historical society,"

Louella explained. Her hat bobbed over the severe bun of thick gray hair on the back of her head.

"Yes, indeed," Florie said enthusiastically, her lined face a softer version of her sister's once-pretty features. "But we are a bit anxious about taking on a project of this size," she admitted. Her hand fluttered at her ample bosom, then lifted nervously to arrange the gray curls that spilled from under her stylish chapeau.

"We hope the proceeds will enable us to produce a history of the area. It's very important to keep our heritage alive, for we have such a rich culture here. It's mostly a German-Swiss influence, and we have some outstanding examples of Victorian architecture," Louella said.

"You'll see that for yourself, though," Amalie told her. "You'll be staying with the Abington sisters. They have a detached apartment that they have put at your disposal."

"That's very kind of you," Milly replied. "I seem to have a small problem, though." She explained about her newly acquired pet, and all the women were equally indignant over Dean Singleton's treatment of Sebastian. To Milly's relief, the Abington sisters assured her that they had no objections to letting her keep one small dog while she stayed in their apartment.

The conversation then turned to the details of the auction. Milly was told that the members of the Altus Historical Society had been actively seeking donations of antique furniture, farm implements, and other household items for the past few months. Quite a few of these items were stored, while others had been promised and merely needed to be picked up. It would be up to Milly to examine the collection, aid in the pickup, and then decide which items would be suitable for the auction. Some would be sold on consignment for the owners, and the historical society would make a commission on the sale.

They discussed the catalog that Milly would compile, as well as the necessary publicity. The committee members were available to help, but Milly soon found that she was expected to be the decision-maker. As amiable as she found this group, Milly had no doubts that the auction would be a success. She simply hoped that Rolfe Hart would not be around much, peering over her shoulder at her every move with that infuriatingly sardonic expression on his face. It would be impossible to work with his overt disapproval.

Milly was perusing the lists of expected items that Amalie had prepared when Rolfe returned. She kept her eyes carefully lowered despite the fact that she knew the second he appeared in the doorway.

"There you are, Rolfe," said his mother. "Come join us. We're very excited about the suggestions Milly has made. With the two of you working together, I know that it will be a wonderful success!"

Milly's head jerked up, and her startled gaze met Rolfe's. He perched on the arm of a flowered chair, looking huge and masculine and terribly out of place in the frilly room. A tremor of alarm traveled down Milly's spine, and her mouth was suddenly dry.

"Did you say—work together?" she asked weakly.

"Didn't I explain? Everything we've gathered is in Rolfe's equipment barn. It's a big metal building with a concrete floor that will be perfect for the auction. People won't mind driving a few miles out of town to attend a big auction, will they?" Amalie asked anxiously. Milly hastened to reassure her that it would not matter.

"Mother wanted to be certain you'd have at least one strong back to help you," Rolfe said. His expression looked as though he had just bitten into one of his own grapes and found it sour. "I was elected."

"Oh! Well, I'm sure that it won't be necessary—I mean . . ." Milly spluttered. She didn't want to appear rude in front of Amalie and the Abington sisters, but working with Rolfe would be intolerable! Within minutes they were certain to be at each other's throats. "That is, I know this is the harvest and I'm sure I could manage—" Rolfe made a negligent gesture that cut off her torrent of words in midstream.

"Relax. I'm sure that I can find a few minutes here and there to help out my own mother." His meaning was crystal clear, and Milly began to fume. He'd help his mother, all right, but he made it plain that his being with Milly was under duress!

"Besides, Milly," Amalie said, "Rolfe knows the area like the back of his hand, and you'll have to use his truck to pick up the things we've been promised."

"Oh, I see," Milly murmured. There seemed to be no graceful way to avoid Rolfe's company. "Well, in that case, I appreciate the help." The words threatened to clog Milly's throat but she forced them out, trying to appear civil despite the fact that she'd like to smack Rolfe's smug face as he enjoyed her discomfiture!

"I can manage some free time tomorrow, so we'll get started right away," Rolfe said.

Milly ground her teeth. It was obvious he wanted to be free of her just as fast as he could, and although she felt the same, it rankled that he found her so unattractive. Or was it that he hadn't forgiven her for their first encounter? It was all so confusing!

"In that case, you'll probably want to get settled in right away," Louella said, producing a key from her handbag. "Sister and I have a bit of shopping to do

36

before we return home. Would you mind finding your own way? The apartment is over the garage."

Rolfe reached out and took the key. "I'll take Milly over there," he said.

"I'm sure I can find it if someone will direct me. May I have the key, please?" she asked, too sweetly. She clenched her teeth and forced a pleasant smile as Rolfe absently tossed the key and caught it several times.

"It's too far to walk."

"I'm in my jeep," she pointed out, then frowned as Rolfe slowly shook his head.

"I had the garage pick it up so the taillight could be repaired," he said.

"You what?" Milly said shrilly. Rage poured through her at his high-handed actions, but she refused to disgrace herself in front of her new friends. Mentally she counted to ten, recited three tongue-twisters, considered innovative ways to commit mayhem on Rolfe Hart, then forced her lips into the semblance of a smile. "How very thoughtful," she croaked.

"I thought so," Rolfe said smugly. Milly gritted her teeth to keep from screaming. "Come on. I'll run you over there right now."

Milly forced herself to bid the women a cordial good-bye, then followed Rolfe out, stopping in the kitchen to pick up Sebastian. She held the puppy on her lap as she rode in Rolfe's blue truck, staring stonily out the windshield. The silence stretched between them as Rolfe negotiated the narrow streets.

"Nothing to say?" he asked. He was baiting her, and she knew it.

"You want me to thank you for taking away my transportation?" she snapped.

"I was concerned for your safety."

37

"Fiddlesticks! You just wanted your own way, and you couldn't get it except by going behind my back! Well, let me tell you something, Mr. Hart, I don't like being controlled by you!"

Rolfe looked at Milly, noting the seductive pout of her lower lip. He ran a hand over his jaw in consternation. Why did she have to be so prickly, sitting there all slender and sexy in her tight jeans? He had merely thought to save her some trouble. Indeed, he felt obligated to see the jeep repaired since the damage had been his fault. It was obvious that she needed someone to look after her. Why was she so reluctant to accept his help? It made Rolfe uncomfortable to see the coolness on her normally animated face.

He cleared his throat. "Perhaps I was a bit hasty," he ventured.

Milly shot him a mocking look. "Perhaps? And how am I going to get around while I'm here? I can't even go get anything to eat!"

"I'll pick you up tomorrow, so you won't even need your jeep. They'll have it fixed in a few days. And I took the liberty of picking up a few groceries for you," he said, jerking a thumb to indicate the truck bed.

Milly struggled with a complexity of emotions. She supposed she ought to be pleased at his thoughtfulness, but the way he treated her like an incompetent infuriated her anew.

"You did? You're doing it again—treating me like some helpless baby! Well, let me tell you—Oh, my goodness!"

Milly's mouth fell open in amazement as Rolfe pulled up in the drive of the Abington house, a three-storied Victorian mansion adorned like an elaborate white wedding cake with gingerbread trim icing. The delicate filigree of carved fretwork and turned spools

38

reflected the sun brightly, casting complicated patterns of shadow against the painted siding.

"Pretty, isn't it?" he asked.

Milly had forgotten her annoyance. "It's magnificent!" she breathed, her eyes sparkling.

"I'm sure Miss Louella and Miss Florie will give you a tour. I'll show you where you're to stay." They parked the truck, then Rolfe grabbed Milly's suitcases from the rear of the truck and handed her the bag of groceries. He led her up a narrow staircase on the side of the garage. He produced the key, unlocked the door, then let her enter the apartment first.

Milly surveyed her new domain with pleasure and surprise. She set her bag on a tiny wire ice cream parlor table that served as a dining room, then she and Sebastian made a brief tour. The apartment was merely two rooms and a bath, but it was surprisingly comfortable, for all the eccentricity of its dowager furnishings. A slick horsehair sofa and wicker rocker lined the wall opposite the table. The table had two matching wire chairs, and a tiny kitchen hid behind double louver doors. A charming sleigh bed topped with a crocheted granny square spread nearly filled the small bedroom, but the bath was a surprise, for it contained a pedestal basin and an old-fashioned footed tub that Milly could not wait to try. Dormers sprouted from unexpected angles, revealing windows with enchanting vistas. From where she stood Milly could see the geometric beds of the gardens between the garage and the back of the house. Out the bedroom windows lay terraced vineyards, green with summer growth. Sebastian, worn out from his busy day, circled a small kitchen rug, then curled up on it to nap.

"Not bad," Rolfe muttered, inspecting the room. He carried Milly's suitcases into the tiny bedroom and set them at the foot of the bed. When he turned, he found her watching him with a strange expression on her face. She seemed lost in thought, but she jerked to awareness when he raised a questioning eyebrow.

"What? Oh, yes. It's very nice. I'm sure I'll be comfortable here," Milly said, stumbling over her words. She had been inwardly marveling at how Rolfe's lean form and almost tangible virility seemed to shrink the room. The path her thoughts were taking was very disconcerting.

"Well, I'll let you get settled," Rolfe said, moving toward the door. "I'll pick you up at about nine tomorrow morning, okay?"

"Sure." Milly nodded as she followed him. "Uh, Rolfe? Haven't you forgotten something?" He paused at the door, puzzled, as she held out her hand. "My key, please," she said softly.

"Oh!" Rolfe dug deep into the pocket of his khaki pants and pulled out the key. He let it dangle over Milly's palm for a moment. Their eyes met, and Milly felt an excited tingle creep along her skin. Rolfe's mouth twisted into a crooked grin and he dropped the key into her hand, curling her fingers closed with his own. His voice was husky when he spoke, and his words shoved Milly's heart rate into overdrive.

"It might be too much of a temptation, at that."

CHAPTER THREE

Milly accepted a second cup of coffee from Louella Abington and sat back in the creaking wicker armchair with a sigh of contentment.

"This is a glorious way to start the day," Milly said with a smile. "Thank you for inviting me." Florie had knocked on Milly's door early to invite her to breakfast with them in the sun room at the rear of the old house. Sunday morning was a quiet time in Altus, and the sisters spent a leisurely few hours before they attended church services.

"It's so nice to have a young person visit," Florie said. Her plump shape was hidden under an old-fashioned bibbed apron while she cleared the remains of the meal.

"And thank you for showing me the house," Milly added. She cradled the cup in both hands and allowed the warm aroma of the coffee to fill her nostrils.

"We enjoy showing it off," Louella remarked, crisply folding the Sunday paper. "Although it has been difficult keeping it up since Papa died. Old houses, you know," she added with a vague gesture that was meant to explain everything.

But Milly did know, and sympathized. As the women had shown her through their home, it had become apparent that the house was a bit like the Abington sisters themselves—genteel and charming, but beginning to show its age nonetheless. Milly's expert eye had spotted the warped floorboards, the gently peeling paint, the faded wallpaper. It took money to support a home of this size and age, and that was a commodity evidently in short supply for the Abington sisters.

The women could hardly use all of the enormous house, so much of it was shut up, while the furnishings that crammed the many unoccupied rooms were draped in sepulchral dust sheets. The living portion of the house retained a Victorian atmosphere, complete with Turkey carpets, rosewood settees, and frayed velvet draperies. Milly longed to see it restored to its former glory, windowpanes shining and crisp white curtains drifting in the mountain air. It would take a large family to fill it up, but Milly could almost hear the laughter of children playing on the wide porches. It was a fantasy particularly poignant since an identical one had sustained Milly during her own lonely childhood. She shook her head to clear away the hazy picture as Rolfe's blue truck pulled into the driveway.

"There's my ride, ladies," she said, putting down her cup.

"And you'll try to come to church with us next Sunday, won't you?" Florie asked expectantly.

"I'd love to," Milly said, her voice warm. "But today I'm at Rolfe's disposal, so I'd better go."

She hurried out the back door, calling to Rolfe as he walked toward the garage stairs. Rolfe turned at her call, then stood still, momentarily stunned by Milly's bright face. He had never seen anyone so vibrantly alive. Every move she made was full of suppressed energy, and the happy smile she wore bubbled over with joy. It was hard not to respond to such animation, but Rolfe scowled and fought the surge of attraction. He wasn't interested in a romantic relationship right now, he told himself firmly. When the time came, he'd find someone honest, solid, and dependable, not a nitwit like Milly Carter!

Milly hesitated, her steps faltering at the thunderous expression that crossed Rolfe's face when he saw her. Inwardly she sighed, disappointed that after their almost friendly farewell of yesterday, he had reverted back to frowning disapproval. She smoothed suddenly nervous hands down her neat slacks and lime green knit shirt, and clutched her purse and notebook tighter. She'd do her best not to antagonize the beast today, she decided.

"Good morning, Rolfe," she said sedately.

"Hi." Rolfe tore his frozen gaze away from her fresh face and tender lips long enough to wave at the Abington sisters. "Let's go," he said curtly. He was surprised at the sharp pang he felt as he watched the light die behind her lovely eyes.

"Pretty day," Milly murmured once they were on their way in the truck.

"Yeah."

She tried again. "Been up long?"

Rolfe arched a sandy eyebrow at this. "Since dawn. We're harvesting, you know."

"Oh."

She was so subdued that Rolfe felt a surge of guilt that he had been so brusque. After all, it wasn't Milly's fault that he found her so attractive he had to fight it. It wouldn't hurt to be a bit more friendly, he thought.

"We'll be driving right past where my crew is working, so you'll see how it's done," he offered. Then he began to talk easily of the process, how they used harvesting machines as well as laborers, and how the grapes were then sent to the crushers at the winery. He told her the crusher removed the stems; then the

43

must—the pulp, skins, juice, and seeds—was sent to a tank for a few days to develop color and esters.

"Then is it wine?" Milly asked, interested in spite of herself.

"Not yet," Rolfe replied with a smile, warming to his favorite subject. "We drain the juice and send it to the tanks in the fermenting room to age for a while; then it's bottled. I'll take you for a tour sometime while you're here if you'd like."

"Thank you, I'd enjoy that," Milly replied. She was a bit surprised at the offer, but it was obvious that Rolfe enjoyed his work and talking about it had mellowed his mood.

Rolfe turned the truck off the main road and headed up into the rolling countryside. He pointed out the cloud of dust in a vineyard that indicated the harvesting. Milly watched the industrious workers moving swiftly up and down the terraced rows. Presently Rolfe turned off to another narrow lane lined with vineyards, passed a small white farmhouse surrounded by trees, then pulled up to a large metal shed about the size of a small gymnasium.

"Here we are," he announced.

Milly looked about her with interest. "This is perfect!" she said. Her natural enthusiasm began to surface again as she pictured the auction taking place here. There was plenty of parking space, a few shady trees to lounge under, and the open-air shed would provide plenty of room to display the sale items as well as set up chairs for the audience.

"I'll show you the things we've collected," Rolfe said. They made their way into the dim interior of the huge barn. It took Milly's eyes a minute to adjust to the dimness after the bright sun outside. Blinking, she noticed the empty spaces along the walls where various pieces of heavy machinery were meant to go.

There were wagons for hauling grapes lined up on the far end, and out the back Milly could see more fields of grape vines.

Rolfe removed a huge plastic tarp to reveal chests and chairs, bric-a-brac, and boxes of miscellaneous items stacked haphazardly against the wall of the shed.

"Amalie has been busy!" Milly laughed, slightly taken aback by the number and assortment of items.

Rolfe nodded, his mouth twisted wryly. "These things over here belong to Mother," he said. "I think she wants them sold on consignment." Milly nodded, making a mental note. There were several fine pieces, and she couldn't blame Amalie for wanting to make a little money herself. Although she was a widow of comfortable means, she certainly didn't appear overly affluent. Winemaking must not be a very lucrative business, she supposed.

"Where do you want to start?" he asked.

Milly threaded a hand through her glossy brown hair and stared at the stack for a moment. Then she shrugged.

"At the beginning, I suppose. Look, Rolfe, I know you're busy. Why don't you let me poke through this stuff by myself for a while. I can double-check Amalie's list and write out some descriptions. I'll wait until you come back to help me with anything I can't get to."

"Well, there are a few things I need to check on," he admitted. "If you're sure—"

"I'm positive! It's going to take me some time to go through all this."

"Okay. I'll be back in a couple of hours. We can get some lunch, then we'll ride out and see about picking up those other items. Most folks will be home on a Sunday afternoon."

45

"That sounds fine!" she said, and waved him away, eager to begin.

During the next two hours Milly inspected all the items, hastily scribbling a description of each in her notebook and assigning it a number. There was a wide assortment, some of it quality stuff, some of it junk. There were heavy mahogany dressers, bedsteads, and chifforobes. There were kerosene lanterns, sets of china, and old plows. Rocking chairs with horsehide seats sat next to delicate bentwood chairs and a velvet-covered chaise. There was even a moose head trophy and several moth-eaten rugs.

Milly had to move things around to reach some of the items buried under the stacks of boxes. She found boxes that contained sets of delicately colored Depression and Carnival glass and knew these avidly collected items would sell well. There was a collection of antique buttons and several old guns, including a vintage musket.

As she moved down the row, Milly left a trail of rearranged boxes and chairs, things she had set out of her way as she worked. Despite the protection inside the shed and the cool cement floor, the summer heat had worked its way inside and Milly was flushed from her exertions. There was a smudge of dirt on her cheek, and her hands were filthy from handling the dusty array. Despite it all, she was enjoying herself thoroughly.

One of the largest items was a tall armoire the size of a small bedroom. Its double doors were tied shut with a rope that looped over the top. Milly suspected that it might contain clothes or dishes, but she couldn't open it with that rope wrapped around it. Unfortunately, the rope seemed to be tied on top of the darned thing. Milly chewed her lips for a moment as she studied the situation. Then she dragged a sturdy wooden kitchen chair over to the armoire. She climbed up on the seat but still couldn't reach the knotted end of the rope. Gingerly she took hold of the protruding cornice, then placed her toes on the back of the chair and scrambled up on top of the armoire.

As she pulled herself onto the top, the chair wobbled, then clattered over onto its side, leaving her stranded. Milly balanced herself by holding on to a steel I-beam that supported the building. She was a lot higher than she had expected. She grumbled silently to herself, then got to her knees and began trying to unknot the stubborn hemp rope. She hoped she could climb down off this thing without turning it over, too.

"What are you doing up there?" Rolfe's voice startled Milly and she jumped and swayed, catching her balance on the beam once more. She glared furiously down at Rolfe.

"Are you trying to give me a heart attack?" she gasped.

"Get down from there before you break your fool neck!" he roared.

"I'm trying to untie this rope," she explained in her most reasonable tone of voice. She peered over the edge of the armoire into Rolfe's purpling countenance and wondered what she'd done this time to enrage him so.

"I'll cut the damn rope!" he hollered. "Now get down!"

"All right, all right!" Milly muttered. "Would you be so kind as to set up that chair for me?" Rolfe placed the chair upright, then Milly tried to slide off the top on her stomach, but her toes dangled helplessly several inches shy of the chair seat. She had almost decided just to let go when she felt two warm hands on her rib cage.

"I've got you," Rolfe said. He easily supported her

47

until her feet touched the chair. Then she turned and he lifted her by the waist and set her on her feet in front of him.

"Thanks," Milly said breathlessly. She cast a timid glance at him to see if he was still angry, but he was looking at her with a tender, bemused expression. Milly blinked, suddenly very conscious of his hands still at her waist and the proximity of his masculine bulk.

"What's the matter? Do I have mud on my face?" she asked with a nervous little laugh.

The corner of Rolfe's mouth twitched. Now that Milly was safe, he could relax again. When he had seen her on top of the armoire, he had felt certain that her impetuosity was going to get her hurt this time. He didn't dwell too long on the reason that had blown away his typical cool control.

"As a matter of fact, you do," he said. With his thumb he gently rubbed the smudge on her cheekbone. Milly swallowed, her pulse jumping at the intimate ministration.

"I'm a mess." She half-laughed, brushing at the tangle of her hair.

Rolfe shook his head, his expression solemn. "A gorgeous mess," he said. His blue eyes were vivid in the tan of his face, and Milly knew that he was going to kiss her. And suddenly she knew that she wanted him to kiss her, very badly. It was a sharp disappointment when Rolfe resolutely set her away from him, his face suddenly closed and placid once more.

"I'll take you to the house to clean up," he said.

Milly turned away to hide her chagrin. Had she misread him again? Was the chemistry she felt all on her side? How humiliating! What must he think of her? She dusted her dirty hands on the sides of her pants, then noticed the rope.

48

"Are you going to cut this for me?" she asked.

"Oh, sure." He took a pair of sharp clippers from his back pocket, then smoothly severed the hemp. Milly pulled the rope away and opened the doors of the armoire. Her face fell. It contained nothing more than a few old burlap sacks in its cavernous interior. Two disappointments in a row was too much.

"Oh, rats!" she muttered.

"What were you looking for?" Rolfe asked.

Milly picked up a disintegrating sack, then threw it down in disgust. "I don't know. Buried treasure. The Hope Diamond. Plane tickets to Zanzibar," she said flippantly.

"You're nuts, Milly," Rolfe said, shaking his head in wry amusement.

"I know," she said. Nuts to think a man like Rolfe Hart could feel anything but annoyance or disdain for her. She forced a bright smile. "Did you say something about washing up?"

Rolfe drove Milly the short distance back to the white farmhouse they had passed earlier.

"Welcome to my humble abode. Come on in," he urged, leading her up the shallow steps onto the unpainted wooden porch.

"Is this where you live?" Milly asked in surprise. It seemed strange that a formidable individual like Rolfe would live in such a modest home, but it made him more approachable for some reason. As closely as he guarded his emotions, it should be a stone fortress.

"It's comfortable and convenient," he said with an offhanded shrug. "I keep meaning to fix it up a bit, but I never seem to get around to it."

"It's nice." Milly looked with interest at the cozy but shabby living room with its well-worn sofa and what had to be Rolfe's favorite chair sitting before the television. The Sunday newspaper lay scattered on the

49

top of the coffee table, and cluttered bookshelves lined the wall.

"The bath's through there," Rolfe said, pointing down a short hall. "Do you want to pick up something to eat or shall I make us a couple of sandwiches to save time?"

"Sandwiches will do fine," she said. She returned a few minutes later, feeling much better for having washed off the grime and combed her hair. She followed the sounds of cutlery clinking and entered the kitchen. Rolfe turned as she came in, casually kicked closed the refrigerator door, and smiled around the large dill pickle in his mouth. Milly grinned as he handed her two loaded plates.

"Good pickle," Rolfe said, munching. "Want one?"

"No, thanks." Milly giggled. Then she looked at the plates. "Good grief! I can't eat all of this!"

"No? Well, I'll help you. I'm starving. Have a seat," he said, indicating the small breakfast table. Milly inspected the multilayered sandwich on her plate with growing fascination as Rolfe popped the top on a can of beer.

"What do you want to drink? There's beer, milk, cola."

"Cola will do, thanks," she said. He placed her soft drink in front of her. "What, no wine?"

"Certainly not! My creation demands only the finest ale as its accompaniment."

"It's definitely interesting," Milly said. The sandwich, built on a base of french bread, contained ham, cheese, salami, red onion slices and what appeared to be horseradish mustard. Well, she was game. Milly took a bite and chewed thoughtfully as Rolfe waited expectantly. "It's good," she said in surprise.

"What else did you expect? I'm a champion sandwich maker. I've had a lot of practice, since I don't like to cook."

"You should get a wife," Milly mumbled around another mouthful. Rolfe shot her a sharp glance, but she was all innocence, chewing contentedly.

"That takes two," he said.

"Oh, come now, Rolfe," Milly scoffed. "You can't tell me there's not anyone after you. Hardworking, good-looking men are hard to find."

"I've been too busy to notice," he said evasively. Rolfe felt a surge of pleasure. So she thought he was good-looking, did she? Still, it was difficult not to be heart-wary when you'd been burned once before. He pointed at the untouched half of her sandwich. "Are you going to eat that?"

Milly laughed and pushed the plate toward him. "Go ahead." She enjoyed the easy domesticity that had replaced the sizzling awareness between them, although she knew it lurked just below the surface of their polite conversation. The shadow that had briefly crossed Rolfe's face had told her more than he realized. There must have been a woman in Rolfe's past, Milly guessed, someone who had hurt him badly. Milly sipped her drink and mulled this over. Perhaps that explained why Rolfe seemed so aloof. He was a complex man, but one worth knowing, if only he could open himself up to her a little.

"Ready to go?" Rolfe asked. Milly nodded, wondering if she'd ever be able to understand him completely.

They spent the afternoon driving into the backcountry, crossing one name after another off Amalie's neatly typed list as they picked up donations for the auction. Milly enjoyed herself thoroughly, and Rolfe had to admire the way she had with people. His own natural reserve sometimes made it difficult for him to relate easily to others. Milly visited with each person, gleaning interesting tidbits about them all. Even the crustiest old codger opened up for her, and time and again Rolfe spent endless minutes glancing impatiently at his watch while Milly worked her charms.

Rolfe had just loaded an antique trunk into the now-full bed of the pickup when Milly came down the creaky steps of Old Man Creighton's cabin lugging a large jug.

"Look, Rolfe," she said. "Mr. Creighton sent you a gift."

"What?" The old man was an irascible varmint, known far and wide for his mean disposition. Milly had somehow gotten around even him!

"I'm not sure. But I told him you made wine and he grumped a bit and told me to tell you to taste this. Do you think it's moonshine?" Her face was alive with amusement and laughter. "Aren't you going to try it?"

"I don't think—" Rolfe glanced up to see Old Man Creighton standing on the porch with a challenging glint in his eye. Milly watched him expectantly, and Rolfe had the distinct impression that he was being maneuvered ever so gently. Well, he'd prove he could take a joke, too.

Rolfe relieved Milly of the heavy jug and shrugged. "Only one way to find out." He pulled out the cork, sniffed suspiciously, then rolled the jug into position on his arm and took a mouthful. He swallowed, his eyes clenched shut, then he drew a deep, gasping breath. He blinked watering eyes. "Damn, that's good!" he said, his voice hoarse. Milly burst out laughing. Rolfe saluted Creighton, who was grinning in toothless approval. "Best I ever had," Rolfe gasped.

Rolfe was still wiping his watery eyes ten minutes later as they drove back toward Altus.

"You certainly made a friend of Mr. Creighton,"

Milly said with a laugh. "Was it really that good?" she asked.

"Damn near burned off my taste buds," Rolfe said. "You want to try it?"

"Oh, no!" Milly had learned to her grief long ago that she had absolutely no head for alcohol. Even the tiniest amount was her complete undoing. "If it did that to you, I shudder to think what it would do to me!"

They laughed together companionably, and Milly congratulated herself for not having antagonized Rolfe even one time this afternoon. She gave a little sigh of happiness and enjoyed the scenic beauty of the rolling countryside.

"Tired?" Rolfe asked.

"A little."

"I'll take you home, then. I've got to collect some samples up on St. Mary's mountain."

"Samples?"

"Grapes. I'll have to check the pH to see if we can begin harvesting up there tomorrow."

"Could I come?" Milly asked diffidently.

Rolfe studied her silently. Her eyes were more gray than green, and her dark hair blew gently in the soft breeze. There had been another time, another girl with melting eyes and shining hair. Sweet Monique, the French girl to whom he'd pledged his love, only to have it betrayed. Rolfe's lips thinned with bitter memories. Then he pushed the painful recollections aside.

"Sure, you can come."

Milly wondered what she had done to bring the coolness back to Rolfe's eyes. Their friendly afternoon might never have existed for all the warmth in his words. She sighed again, this time in resignation. How could she learn more about Rolfe if he retreated every time she got too close?

They drove in silence for a few miles, then Rolfe turned up into the hills again, passing the historic St. Mary's Catholic Church from which the mountain took its name. Further along, the vineyards began, sitting in tidy rows on their framework of arbors, the vines outstretched and heavy with clusters of glistening fruit. Rolfe parked the truck near the crest of the hill and Milly got out to admire the vista. She could see the whole town from this vantage. Then she followed Rolfe into the deserted vineyard.

"These are Cynthiana grapes," he said as they walked. "It's a native Arkansas variety and I think it makes the best wine." He paused before a loaded vine that stood higher than his head. His hands worked among the clusters of wine-red grapes, lifting them tenderly.

"These are different," she said, pointing to another variety of grape of the palest green.

"We sell them for table grapes," he explained, coming up beside her. He clipped off a succulent bunch. "Try them. They're seedless. Of course, if we have extra, they also make an excellent white wine."

"Mmm!" Milly bit into the juicy flesh of the sweet, sun-warmed fruit. "Delicious!"

Rolfe clipped samples from the top, middle, and sides of the vine, slipping them into a small bag; then he moved further down the row and repeated the procedure. The earth was well tilled, completely free of weeds, and Rolfe looked at the twisted stalks of his vines with almost paternal pride.

"You love it, don't you?" Milly asked suddenly.

"Yes, I do," Rolfe said honestly. They had reached an opening at the top of the hill and he scanned the sea of vines with a proprietary air. "The Harts have been on this land for five generations. It's something in my blood. I couldn't do anything else or live anywhere but here."

"What a lucky man you are," Milly said softly. Never had she felt the kind of strong family bonds that held Rolfe, gave him his roots and his identity. She could envy him without malice, but her face was wistful. She turned away.

"Milly?" Rolfe's hand on her shoulder stopped her, turned her back to face him. There was a perplexed frown between his brows as he struggled to comprehend her expression, or perhaps himself. She quivered under his touch and knew that he felt it.

He groaned and gathered her close. "God, Milly! I know I shouldn't kiss you, but I can't help myself," he said, his voice husky.

"Why shouldn't you?" she asked. She was suddenly breathless, her arms clasped around his waist for support because she feared she would melt into his warmth.

He shook his head in bewilderment. "I don't know. I can't think of anything right now except how much I want to kiss you."

"You wanted to before and didn't," she murmured, remembering the morning.

"That was a long time ago, and I seem to have lost my self-control since then."

"Is it important?" she whispered.

Rolfe slowly shook his head. "Not at the moment."

He bent his head, and his lips met hers in a soft and tender exploration that took Milly's breath. Her heart pounded out of control as his thumb caressed the soft underside of her jaw, tilting her head to meet his mouth more fully.

Milly's lips opened under his persuasion, sharing without reservation the soft inner secrets. Her mouth tasted of grapes, sweet and fruity, and Rolfe's tongue explored the delicate recesses as though savoring the flavor of his harvest.

A soft breeze rustled the grape leaves, and the drone of insects sounded on the hot summer air, but nothing penetrated their concentration on each other. Milly felt only the strength of Rolfe's lean body as her hands explored the exciting outline of muscles along his back. His arm wrapped about her waist, drawing her ever closer, and his other hand smoothed the thick tresses at the nape of her neck.

Milly was a quivering mass of pure sensation, mindless with an aching need evoked by Rolfe's hands and lips. His mouth left hers to trail across her cheekbone, her temple, the feathered tips of her eyelids. Eyes closed, Milly lifted softly parted lips, blindly seeking the solace of his mouth until at last he reclaimed her.

This kiss was different, no longer exploring but demanding with a burning hunger that threatened to flame out of control. Milly returned his fire, responding to Rolfe with all the spontaneity and generosity of her loving nature.

When the kiss ended, they were both shaken by the ferocity of their emotions. They stared at each other, breathing hard.

"It's a good thing we're in the middle of a vineyard, or I might be tempted to do something we'd both regret," Rolfe said at last, straining for lightness.

Stung, Milly broke free from his arms and glared at him. Why did he fight so hard against feelings that were so right?

"For once in your life, Rolfe," she snapped, "it wouldn't hurt you to do something impulsive! Too bad it's too late to find out what!"

CHAPTER FOUR

"No, Sebastian, you bad dog!" Milly scolded. Sebastian looked up, the remains of a petunia on his muddy snout, then unconcernedly returned to the absorbing task of demolishing the Abington sisters' flower beds. Milly shuffled the stack of catalog descriptions she had been working on into a neat pile and placed them on her lawn chair, then hurried across the yard to the busy puppy. She hoped she could repair the damage before anyone appeared, but it was already too late. Roger Buford, the Abington sisters' venerable gardener and chauffeur, had just turned the corner of the house.

"Oh, Buford! I'm sorry!" Milly hastened to apologize. Buford stared morosely at the new damage. He and Sebastian had been having a running battle all week, and Buford knew when he was beaten. The toothpick that inevitably jutted from his mouth shifted from one corner to the other.

"I guess it was time to replace them petoonies anyhow," he said sadly in his gravelly monotone.

"I'll help you," Milly offered swiftly. She swatted Sebastian and sternly ordered him out of the flowers. The puppy responded to the tone of her voice and retreated, tail between his legs. He took up a position under her vacant chair and watched his mistress with soulful, accusing eyes. "I'm trying to make him understand, really I am," she said. "He's just too young to have any manners yet."

"Just like all kids nowadays," Buford muttered. He gauged the damage to his precious flowers, then sighed. "Guess I could put in some marigolds. Miss Florie's right partial to marigolds."

"Just tell me what to do," Milly said eagerly. She liked the older man, despite his surly manner. Florie had confided that Buford had been with them since they were both quite young and now was more or less their overseer for the few remaining acres of family vineyards. He owned his own small house set on a lot near the vineyards and received a pension, but he steadfastly ignored any suggestions that he retire. Milly heartily approved of the way Buford took care of his charges, looking after the house and grounds and seeing the women safely in and out of their antique sedan on an occasional shopping trip.

Milly soon found herself on her hands and knees beside Buford, wielding a sturdy trowel as they repaired the ravages to the flower bed. Milly dug as enthusiastically as Sebastian had. She had never had much of a chance to try her hand at any sort of gardening, so the experience was a novel and pleasant one. The fecund odor of the rich soil rose to tickle her nose, and the dirt felt warm and alive between her fingers. She could begin to see why producing things from the earth held such fascination for Rolfe.

Milly frowned and stuck her trowel deep into the loamy dirt with unnecessary force. Rolfe's behavior for this past week had totally perplexed her. They had been together a great deal, since her jeep was still in the garage waiting for a part, but there had been no repeat of the passionate kiss they had shared in the vineyard. Instead, Rolfe kept her at arm's length, his every action that of the perfect gentleman, but so cool

58

and aloof that Milly had begun to fear she had imagined the whole incident.

She supposed she should be grateful that Rolfe had taken this particular decision out of her hands. It still made her cheeks burn to remember how she had responded so uninhibitedly to his kiss. If his mere touch could intoxicate her senses, it certainly would be wiser to keep her distance. Besides, she didn't know if her emotional state was strong enough to withstand Rolfe's vacillations in attitude toward her. He drew her close, only to push her away. Despite the undeniable attraction between them, Milly decided that she had to be reasonable, too. She'd be courteous and coolly friendly, but she wouldn't let things get out of hand again. When the time came for her to leave Altus, her heart would be intact.

Her attention was caught by a low droning in the distance that grew steadily louder. "What on earth is that?" she asked Buford. She sat back on her heels, carelessly wiping her dirty palms on her shorts. Buford grimaced and shot a glance skyward.

"Crazy fools," he muttered. He took the toothpick from his mouth and gestured toward the sound. "Got a new way to break their necks."

"What?"

"Bunch of the young fellers 'round here learning to fly them little bitty one-man planes and 'copters and such. Dern fools!" he denounced.

Milly hid a smile. It wouldn't do to tell Buford it sounded like fun to her!

"Milly!" Florie Abington waved to her from the back porch. "Rolfe's here, dear." Milly stood and hastily rinsed the dirt from her hands with a garden hose.

"I'll be right there," she called. Rolfe had promised to take her back out to the storage shed this afternoon.

59

Her pace quickened unconsciously, and she bounded up the porch steps.

Rolfe stood in the broad hall talking to Florie. The sight of him never failed to stir Milly's senses. He listened to the older woman with an expression of affection on his handsome face, his hands tucked palms up into the back pockets of his jeans in a typically male stance. His white shirt was open at the neck, revealing the tanned column of his throat. A few golden chest hairs curled at the edge of the opening, and Milly's fingers tingled with the urge to stroke their softness, sending her earlier resolutions right out the window.

Rolfe turned as she approached, his expression unsmiling. "Ready to go?" he asked.

Rolfe found it hard to form the words around the sudden constriction in his throat. In brief tan shorts, plaid shirt, and sandals, Milly looked delectable. Her slim legs were long and shapely, and there was a wholesomeness about her sun-kissed face that he knew belied her passionate nature. He thrust that unsettling memory away. From now until the auction his relationship with Milly must remain strictly business, for his own peace of mind.

"Ready when you are," Milly replied now.

"Oh, Rolfe," Florie said, "could you take that old Victrola out to the shed today?"

Rolfe was glad of anything that would take his mind off Milly. "Sure thing," he said.

"It's upstairs. Come along, I'll show you," Florie said. She and Rolfe headed for the staircase, followed by Milly. The phone that sat on a table in the hall suddenly pealed. "Will you get that, Milly?"

"Certainly." Milly picked up the receiver. "Hello?"

"Is this the Abington residence?" asked a voice.

"Yes, it is," Milly replied.

"Milly? Is that you?"

"Gareth!" Milly's face lit up as she recognized the voice of her friend and attorney, Gareth Ott. "It's good to hear from you!"

"Do you realize how long I've been trying to get in touch with you? And how much trouble it's been?" Gareth asked irritably.

Milly laughed softly. She could almost imagine Gareth pushing his wire-rimmed glasses higher on the bridge of his aquiline nose and running his hands through his hair in exasperation.

"Now, Gareth, I have a perfectly good mailing address in Hot Springs. You should try writing."

"I might point out that since you only seem to check it once a year that doesn't really do me much good," Gareth said.

"Don't grumble at me." Milly laughed. "How's Sara and the kids?"

"Fine, fine. But listen, Milly, you really have got Jonathan in a tizzy this time."

"Jonathan?" Milly asked. Jonathan Marshall was chairman of the board of Carter Petroleum. "What have I done to Jonathan?"

"Nothing. That's the problem. You've got to come to Little Rock for the next stockholders' meeting."

"But Gareth, I don't want to," Milly explained sweetly. "That's what I've got you and Jonathan for, isn't it?" Milly's business interests were ably administered by a trusted staff, and the Carter Foundation found many philanthropic causes worthy of their attention.

"Jonathan is adamant this time. You must put in an appearance." He named a date just two weeks away.

"Impossible," Milly said. "I'm working, and besides, my jeep is in the shop. I have no way to get there."

"Damnit, Milly!" Gareth shouted. Milly had to pull

61

her ear away from the receiver. "Why do you insist on driving that death trap when you have a perfectly fine Mercedes sitting in your driveway here? I'll have one of the men drive it up for you."

"No! Don't do that! That car belonged to Howard. You know how I feel about things like that!" Milly said. Although she had nothing to hide, she preferred to keep a low profile where her wealth was concerned. She couldn't stand it if the new friends she had made in Altus suddenly changed the way they treated her. Oh, they wouldn't mean to, of course, but there was something about being worth millions that was slightly off-putting to the average individual.

Milly had learned through hard experience how things could change. At eighteen she had thought herself desperately in love with a young man who had turned out to be just another fortune hunter, exactly as Cousin Howard had predicted. The near-disastrous encounter had left Milly wary. Her money had provided for her physical comforts but burdened her with loneliness. Since possessions had never meant much to her, it simplified her life as an itinerant auctioneer to pretend she was no different from the next person.

Milly heard Florie and Rolfe coming back down the stairs. "I've got to go now," she said into the receiver. "Tell Jonathan not to look for me! Bye, Gareth!" His shouted protest was silenced as she hung up. Before her fingers released the phone, however, it rang again. Milly snatched it up.

"I can't talk," she hissed, gazing anxiously toward the stairs. "I'm not coming, and I don't want the Mercedes!" She slammed the phone down just as Rolfe appeared at the bottom of the steps carrying a bulky wicker chest that housed the old Victrola.

"I'll get the door for you, Rolfe, dear," Florie said,

hastening toward the front entrance. "Who was that on the phone, Milly?"

"Uh—wrong number," Milly answered brightly.

Rolfe maneuvered the bulky object across the wide front porch toward his truck. Milly would have followed them, but the phone once again shrilled loudly. Milly gazed at the object in exasperation. She shot a quick glance out the front door and saw Florie and Rolfe at the truck. She snatched up the receiver.

"Gareth, can't you take no for an answer?" she snapped.

"Ah, beg your pardon," came a hesitant male voice. "Is this the Abington residence?"

Milly flushed scarlet as she realized the caller wasn't Gareth at all! "Oh, sorry! Yes, it is. I thought . . ." she tried to explain.

"Is Miss Louella Abington there?" the man demanded.

"No, she's out visiting," Milly explained. "But her sister is here."

"Just take a message, please," the man said sternly. "This is Carl Jenkins from the bank. Tell Miss Louella I must speak with her first thing in the morning regarding the past-due mortgage on their vineyards. I've been waiting all week for their call. It's imperative I talk with her tomorrow. Is that clear?"

"Yes, sir," Milly said, a little frown pleating her forehead. A past-due mortgage? That sounded ominous for the Abington sisters. "I'll give her the message," she promised, scribbling a note on a nearby pad. She replaced the receiver and stared pensively at the writing. She jumped as the phone rang under her hand once more.

"Yes?"

"Don't you hang up on me again, Milly!" Gareth ordered. "We've got to settle a few things!"

"Gareth, please!" Milly cried. She could see Rolfe heading back up the front porch steps. "I can't talk now!"

"Talk, or I'll show up on your doorstep driving that damned Mercedes!" he threatened.

"All right! What?" Milly demanded, biting her lip.

"You must come to Little Rock. There are documents to be signed, as well as the meeting, and Jonathan to pacify."

"I can't!" Milly wailed. "Not until after the auction!"

"Oh, all right," Gareth snapped. "When's the auction?" Milly told him. "Then I'll convince Jonathan to reschedule the stockholders' meeting for the day following that. You be there, is that understood?"

"Yes, I can do that," Milly said, breathing a sigh of relief.

"And no Mercedes," he promised, his good humor returning now that he had gotten his way.

Milly grinned. "No Mercedes," she agreed. "Goodbye."

"Wrong number again?" Rolfe asked. Milly spun around, trying not to look guilty. "Mercedes McCormick lives down the street," he continued. "I wonder if that's who the caller wanted."

"No Mercedes here," she said, shrugging. If she wasn't asked any questions, then she wouldn't have to give any incriminating answers, she reasoned. She rubbed her hands nervously on her shorts and abruptly changed the subject. "Rolfe, when is my jeep going to be fixed? That garage has taken long enough. I think I'll go over there and check on it myself."

"No, don't do that," Rolfe said hastily. "I talked with them just yesterday. You know how it is in a small town."

64

"I hate having to inconvenience you every time I need to do something!"

"It's no problem," Rolfe said gruffly. How could he tell Milly that her dependency on him was one way he could keep tabs on her? Knowing her whereabouts gave him a sense of security. At least she couldn't be getting into much trouble if her ability to act on those infuriating, near self-destructive impulses of hers was kept at a minimum! "Are you ready?"

"Let me lock up Sebastian and get my lists." She hurried away, wondering vaguely at Rolfe's puzzling expression. If she hadn't known any better, she'd have sworn it was guilt. But what did Rolfe have to feel guilty about?

By the time Milly and Rolfe finished up at the shed that day, it was well after six o'clock. There was still an abundance of daylight left as the hot summer day stretched into a sultry evening.

"I have to go to the winery," Rolfe said as they headed for his truck. "I need to turn over the tanks. Do you want to come?"

"Sure," Milly said, certain that Rolfe had only made the offer because of his sense of responsibility. Her expression suddenly clouded, and her green eyes were puzzled. "But how do you turn over a tank? I thought you told me they were very big!"

Rolfe stared down into Milly's concerned face for a moment, then reluctantly began to chuckle. "I don't literally turn it over," he said with a laugh, shaking his head. "Big is an understatement. They each hold about six thousand gallons of juice. I forget I'm dealing with a layman. I'll show you what I mean when we get there."

Rolfe drove back into Altus, turned up a side street, then pulled into a drive that led to a group of buildings. In neat lettering over the main entrance was the inscription, Hart Familie Vinery. Soon Milly was following Rolfe through a confusing complex that included enormous redwood and stainless steel tanks, a laboratory, a work yard, bottling and labeling areas, and showrooms. He explained that turning over a tank simply meant pumping the juice from the bottom of a tank back to the top, where the "cap" of skins floated on the surface. This helped produce color and flavor in a developing wine. Milly watched as Rolfe manipulated the two-inch hose over the top of a huge tank.

"Five minutes at a time is all it takes," Rolfe explained as he completed his task. "We'll be through with the grape harvest in another two weeks, but the wine-making process goes on into October. We cool the juice, allow it to ferment for one to five weeks, then we filter it, add the fining agents to remove proteins, then bottle it. We even make a by-product by crystallizing out the potassium tartrates."

"What's that?" Milly asked.

Rolfe grinned. "Ever heard of cream of tartar?"

Milly was astounded. "I've used that in pie meringues. I didn't know it came from grapes!"

Milly was fascinated by everything she saw and asked innumerable questions. Rolfe proved an apt instructor, lecturing his captive audience and loading Milly with all sorts of technical information. Her head was spinning with facts and figures by the time they returned to the showrooms, but she had enjoyed herself thoroughly. It was clear that Rolfe loved every aspect of his work, for he talked about it with enthusiasm.

At one point Milly had actually stopped trying to absorb all the information and merely studied Rolfe as he talked. His blue eyes glowed and he gestured animatedly, his pride in what he was accomplishing evident. Milly studied the square line of his stubborn jaw, the jut of his cheekbones, and knew that here was a man determined to succeed. The pride of five generations flowed through him as strong as the rich red wine he made, and he would not fail in his stewardship of the land and its bounty.

"Here, I'll show you what I mean," Rolfe was saying now. Milly brought her attention back at these words. They stood in the showroom, where cases of bottles of every conceivable variety of wine were stacked. He moved behind a long oak bar and began to set out various bottles of wine. Before she could protest, he filled a little paper cup with a deep red wine and held it out to her. "This is the Cynthiana. See how you like it," he said.

Milly hesitated, cursing her awkward metabolism that sent liquor straight to her head. It would be churlish to refuse, she decided, and besides, it really was a tiny cup. She took a tentative sip, then another.

"It's good," she praised.

"Dry, but robust," he agreed. He poured from another bottle. "But try this one next. It's our Burgundy Dry. Swirl it around and then smell the bouquet. How do you think they compare?"

Milly took a deep breath, then gamely sampled the second cup.

"I *can* tell a difference!" she said in surprise.

Rolfe nodded approvingly. "Good, but don't just sip it. You have taste buds everywhere in your mouth. Don't deprive any of them. Roll the wine around in your mouth to pick up all the flavor, like this," he said, demonstrating.

Milly forced back a giggle as Rolfe seemed to chew a mouthful of wine, his expression preoccupied as he studied the flavor. She took another mouthful and tried to emulate his actions, swishing the liquid around inside her mouth. The heady fumes rose through her nose.

"It does make a difference," she agreed dizzily.

"Here, you might enjoy this Seyval Blanc. Most women prefer a white wine." He tipped the bottle toward a clean cup.

"Mmm, I like this one," Milly said, beginning to get the hang of wine tasting. There was a pleasant fuzziness growing behind her ears, and her eyebrows were numb. She pushed her cup back to Rolfe.

"Now this is our Chablis," he said, pouring another sample.

They moved down the counter, sipping little cup after little cup. Rolfe seemed intent on having her taste each variety produced by the Hart Familie Vinery. He lectured her on vintage wines like the Steuben and Cynthiana made from premium varietal grapes, then on varietal wines made from North American and French hybrid grapes. She tasted Delaware, Landot Noir, and Catawba. Then Rolfe brought out the dessert wines: Magnolia, made from the wild muscadine, and a strawberry wine that Milly found fragrant and delicious.

Of course, by this time she thought everything was delicious. She especially thought Rolfe Hart himself delicious. She was fascinated by the sensual curve of his lower lip as he swished and swirled a mouthful of wine. His jaw was stubbled with the shadow of his beard, and she longed to feel the rasp of it against her palms, but she contented herself with just looking at him. His broad shoulders flexed under his white shirt as he deftly applied the corkscrew to yet another bottle, and Milly imagined that those hard muscles must feel like steel encased in velvet.

She leaned against the bar, her elbow bent and her chin propped in her hand. Her eyelids felt incredibly heavy, and a silly little smile curved her lips. She had stopped listening to Rolfe's words long ago, but she loved the timbre of his deep voice even though she had no idea what he was saying. There was a muted roaring in her ears now. She felt so relaxed that she knew she would collapse into a boneless heap if she let go of the bar.

Rolfe searched the racks behind the bar for yet another vintage, his back to Milly. She briefly admired the neat line of his slim hips in his tight jeans, then frowned down into her empty cup and reached for the bottle of strawberry wine. That, too, was disappointingly empty, and she held the bottle up so she could peer down its long neck.

"Is something wrong?" Rolfe asked.

"Hmm?" Milly swayed and smiled, then plunked the bottle back down on the top of the bar. "Nothing at all," she said, enunciating each word carefully because her tongue felt unusually thick. She looked rapturously into his horrified face. "I'm having a wunnerful time!"

"Milly, you're drunk!" Rolfe said slowly.

Milly drew herself up to her full height and tried to look offended. "I most certainly am not! I've only had a few itty-bitty cups. Here, I'll show you, Mr. Rolfe Stick-in-the-Mud Hart!" And she began to count each cup with exaggerated care. "One, two, three—"

"Milly!" Rolfe hurried around the bar to her side. "Why didn't you tell me you had no head for alcohol?"

"You made me lose count," she sighed. "One, two, three . . ."

"Oh, God!" Rolfe groaned. "How could anyone get plastered on such a small amount?"

"Nine, ten, eleven—I am not plastered," Milly said, stacking the paper cups into a swaying tower.

"Like hell," Rolfe muttered. He placed a supporting hand at Milly's waist. "Come on, I'll take you home." Milly set another cup on top of her stack, and the tower toppled over.

"Whee!" she said with a laugh. Her feet seemed unattached to her legs, and she wobbled as Rolfe guided her away from the bar. "Silly old Rolfe." She giggled, smiling up into his disturbed blue eyes. Ignoring his glowering expression, she ran her fingertip down the stubbled line of his jaw, something she had been wanting to do all day.

"You'd better stop that, if you know what's good for you," he said. Milly merely laughed. By this time Rolfe had her at his truck. He picked her up and placed her in the cab. Milly slumped and rested her head on the back of the seat.

Rolfe drove Milly back to her apartment, casting anxious glances her way every few seconds. Her cheeks were flushed and rosy, and she drowsed with her soft lips slightly parted. The tips of her dark lashes cast a fringed shadow across her cheekbones, making her look childlike and vulnerable. Rolfe cursed his lack of foresight. He should have been prepared for one of Milly's stunts. The week had been uneventful, so she was past due for one.

He pulled into the Abington sisters' driveway and parked close to the garage. Rolfe prayed that the women weren't paying any attention to their twilight arrival, because it would be very difficult to explain Milly's condition. He came around to her door.

"Milly? You're home," he said, gently shaking her arm.

Milly opened her eyes. "I'm awake!" she announced, blinking. Her sleepy green eyes focused on Rolfe, and she smiled with such aching tenderness that Rolfe caught his breath.

"Come on," he said gruffly. But Milly's wobbling legs could hardly support her, so with a muffled exclamation Rolfe swept her into his arms and mounted the stairs.

"This really isn't necessary," Milly said, leaning her head trustingly against Rolfe's massive shoulder. It was amazing how secure and protected she felt, but she knew she shouldn't take advantage of him. "I can walk."

"Sure," he agreed sarcastically. He pushed open the door and carried her into the dim apartment. The last rays of the setting sun slanted through the dormer windows, dappling the room. Rolfe dropped Milly's feet to the floor, but his arm remained behind her shoulders to steady her.

"I suggest you get to bed and sleep it off," he said.

Milly tilted her head back to peer into his eyes. Her arms looped lightly around his neck.

"Oh!" she said, mischief glowing in her expression. "Into bed, is it? I knew you couldn't resist my charms. How come it's taken you a whole week to come to your senses, Mr. Rolfe Hart?" A slim fingertip tapped lightly on the end of his straight nose to underscore each word.

"Mil-ly!" Rolfe's tone of warning went unnoticed. Milly's finger traced the inner curves of his ear, her delicate torture sending shivers down Rolfe's spine. Rolfe grasped each of her hands and wrenched them away from his neck.

"Stop, woman!" His breathing was suddenly uneven. "All right, march!" he ordered, turning her around and pointing her toward the bedroom. Milly moved obediently, then swayed as she stood beside the sleigh bed.

Rolfe frowned. "Will you be all right?" he asked.

Milly studied him for a moment, her tongue unconsciously provocative as she licked her dry lips. She looked at him from under hooded lids, shrugged, and gave a little smile.

"Sure," she said. Her hand lifted, and she fanned her fingers at him. "Bye now!"

Rolfe groaned and then sighed in resignation. Well, he'd gotten her into this state; the least he could do was see that she was comfortably tucked into bed. He dropped to one knee and began to loosen the buckles on her sandals. As he slipped one off, then the other, he felt her fingers touch his hair in a soft caress. This was going to be harder than he had expected. He gritted his teeth and stood up. Then his hands moved to the narrow belt buckle at her waist.

"What are you doing?" Milly asked, her tone mildly interested. Rolfe released the zipper, then pushed her shorts down her slim hips.

"Going crazy," he muttered. She wore lace-trimmed bikini panties that peeked out from beneath the wrinkled edge of her plaid shirt. Enough was enough, Rolfe decided. A man could only stand so much. There was no way he was going to take her blouse off, too. She could just sleep in it. "Now get into bed," he ordered hoarsely.

"You're so sweet to take such good care of me," Milly said. Her hands walked up the front of Rolfe's shirt, then tugged at the points of his collar. "Why do you always wear a white shirt?" she asked suddenly. "I mean white's all right, but it's so predictable! Why not blue? Or yellow? I know! Pink! You'd look good in pink!"

"I wouldn't be caught dead in a pink shirt!" Rolfe said, then ground his teeth in exasperation. "Never mind that now!" he ordered curtly.

"Poor Rolfe," Milly said mournfully. "I'll bet you don't have a pink shirt." She gently patted his cheeks in a soothing gesture. She stood on tiptoe, and her full breasts brushed against Rolfe's heaving chest, sending his pulse hammering into his temples. His hands involuntarily steadied her narrow waist while she pressed a sweet, faintly strawberry kiss against his lips.

"Milly, I—oh, hell." Rolfe groaned, then surrendered to the siren's song. His lips eagerly sought the sweetness of Milly's mouth, assuaging a need so elemental in its nature that all thought of propriety was instantly abandoned.

Milly clung to Rolfe, immersed in the symphony of sensations his mobile mouth created on her lips. Pleasure coursed through her, so pure, so strong, that her dreamy state shattered, splintered in a crescendo of desire. Her eyes flew open, and adrenaline surged through her veins, sobering her. The traces of wine evaporated from her foggy brain, only to be replaced by something far more intoxicating.

Rolfe's tongue probed, parted her lips, then played a duet with hers that startled her with its sensuous message. Little sounds came from Milly's throat, and she wove her fingers into his fair hair, holding his head as her breath melded with his in an intimate communication. Rolfe's hands slid beneath the waistband at her hips, pulling her closer into the solid cradle of his thighs and letting Milly feel his need. Breathless excitement made her vibrate like a bowstring in his embrace.

Rolfe groaned, then trailed a fiery path of kisses down her neck as he inhaled the subtle fragrance of her skin. His hands pressed against her hips, massaging the soft mounds and seeking to forge their flesh into one bond. Then he grasped her thigh and lifted her onto the bed, following her down onto the brightly squared afghan. He half-lay across her as his mouth found hers yet again, his tongue hot and devouring in its exploration of the tender inner crevices.

Milly shuddered and moved restlessly against Rolfe, lifting her knee, and his hand caressed the sensitive skin at the back of that joint into singing life. His tongue moved to the corners of her mouth, tasting gently now. Milly shivered, her breath coming in swift pants and her heart racing. She knew she had never wanted any man the way she wanted Rolfe Hart. His merest touch inflamed her so that she couldn't think.

Rolfe's questing hands slipped under her blouse, cupping the lush outline of her breasts within their lacy covering. Milly gasped and moaned when his thumb brushed the tender point of one rounded globe, the nipple contracting into a hard, aroused nub.

Milly's fingers dug into Rolfe's shoulders, and he paused, his face just inches above hers. Their breath mingled as they stared at each other, the planes of Rolfe's face hard with passion, Milly's flushed and soft with lovemaking. Suddenly Rolfe groaned, and without warning he rolled away from her, coming to a seated position on the edge of the bed with his head buried in his hands. Milly felt cold, then hot, as waves of disappointment and humiliation washed over her fevered limbs. She touched his back with a tentative hand, and a jolt of pure pain shot through her as he jerked away.

"Rolfe?"

"God, I'm sorry, Milly," he said, drawing a deep breath. His blue eyes were dark and tortured as he gazed at her hurt expression and quivering lips. "I didn't mean that to happen. I've never taken advantage of a woman who's had too much to drink."

"I'm perfectly sober," Milly said quietly.

"Yeah." Rolfe raked an agitated hand through his

hair, his glance skittering about the room as he fought for composure.

Milly was gazing at him in silent recrimination. How was a man to deal with a woman like that? Rolfe did the only thing he could think of. He caught her abruptly to him and kissed her hard, then released her just as abruptly.

"I'm leaving now, but not because I want to," he said, rising. Milly gazed up at him, her eyes gray-green and cloudy with bewilderment.

"Then why?" she asked, her voice breathy and almost too soft to hear over the beating of her own heart.

"You're one of the most giving, desirable women I've ever known, but I won't seduce you when you've had too much wine and your defenses are down," Rolfe said. "I want you fully aware when I make love to you. And when that time comes, you'll know it, and I'll know it, and nothing will stop us."

Rolfe took a last look at Milly's dumbfounded face, then rose and quietly let himself out of the apartment. Milly sank down on the bed, then grabbed the spread and rolled onto her side into a protective ball. The effects of all the wine she had consumed and the emotional highs and lows of the past few moments combined to produce an unbearable fatigue, but she stared unseeingly at the wall as the import of Rolfe's words hit her.

CHAPTER FIVE

Sebastian's wet tongue licked Milly's fingers, bringing her out of a deep sleep. She groaned and tried to snuggle deeper into the covers, but the persistent pup, hungry for his breakfast, fastened his baby teeth into the cuff of her enveloping nightshirt and growled ferociously. At the same time Milly became aware of a determined knocking on her front door.

"All right, Sebastian, I'm coming," Milly moaned. She was able to sit up on her third try, but her head felt as though it were swollen to five times its normal size. She had managed sometime in the night to crawl to the bathroom to throw up. She'd felt somewhat better after that—at least well enough to change into her nightshirt and curse Rolfe Hart before falling back into bed.

She squinted puffy eyes and wondered what time it was. The knocking continued unabated, so Milly slowly shuffled to the door and flung it open.

"Oh, it's you," she said dully. She left the door open and staggered toward the refrigerator.

"Well, good morning to you, too, sunshine," Rolfe said. He came erect from his lounging position on the doorsill and followed her inside.

"Damn you," she muttered weakly. Her head was pounding too hard for her to yell as she wanted. He was just too damned cheerful for this early in the morning!

"Uh-oh. It's worse than I expected," Rolfe said, his mouth quirked humorously. He shook his head as he noticed her red eyes, tangled hair, and bare feet.

"I'll get you for this," Milly promised darkly.

She painfully poured Sebastian a saucer of milk and tossed a handful of dry puppy food into his dish. She didn't think she could stand the grinding of the electric can opener just yet. Maybe in a week or two, she thought hopefully.

She struggled with the stubborn cap on a glass jar of orange juice until Rolfe took pity on her and unscrewed it, then poured her a glass. Milly glared at him, then sank down on the ice cream parlor chair. One hand covering her aching eyes, she slowly sipped the tart liquid and prayed her jumpy insides would accept it.

"What do you want?" she asked irritably.

"Ever the gracious hostess," Rolfe murmured. Milly gritted her teeth. She had no need for comedy when she was dying. "I thought I'd better check on you after last night," Rolfe explained. He poured himself a glass of orange juice and swallowed it with enjoyment. Milly kept her eyes closed and concentrated on keeping her stomach from disgracing her.

"It's all your fault, anyway," she muttered. Everything was coming back to her now, including the passionate interlude they had shared. How was she going to look this man in the eye in the clear light of day? Suddenly her lips twitched. She kept her face buried in her hand. "If I never see another bottle of strawberry wine, it'll be too soon. What happened after that, anyway?" She peeked at Rolfe through her fingers and was gratified to see his startled expression.

"Don't you remember anything?" he asked.

"Not after the strawberry wine," she said, dropping her hand. "All those little cups . . . I didn't do anything to embarrass you, did I?" she asked guilelessly.

Rolfe's jaw dropped. "Ah, no, no. Everything was fine," he hastened to assure her.

Milly forced back a laugh. No man wanted his prowess as a lover to be so forgettable! Serves him right, she thought, although for exactly what she couldn't be certain—making love to her, not making love to her, getting her drunk, laughing at her hangover.

"Actually," Rolfe continued, "Mother sent me over with a dinner invitation for tonight. Think you'll be up to it?"

"I'll do my best," Milly snapped, then instantly regretted it as her head began a new timpani. "Hand me those aspirin, will you?"

Rolfe opened the small bottle and dropped two white tablets into Milly's outstretched hand. He felt guilty and yet annoyed at her hung-over condition, and irritated that she didn't remember how close they'd come to making love, or his gallant retreat, for that matter. He had spent a restless night remembering plenty and cursing himself for being such a fool.

"Why didn't you tell me you couldn't drink?" he demanded.

"Don't yell at me! I don't recall that you asked. You were too busy lecturing." Milly swallowed the pills and grimaced.

"Of all the dumb stunts! All you had to say was no, thank you!"

"I didn't want to hurt your feelings!" Milly gave an exaggerated sigh. She couldn't resist another dig at Rolfe. "At any rate, at least I was with a man I could trust. Some men ply a girl with liquor, then try to take advantage of her; but you'd never do anything like that. Thanks for seeing me home."

Rolfe nearly choked on his orange juice at Milly's words. Then he looked at her closely. Was she pulling his leg? But no, her distress seemed genuine enough. Rolfe's conscience twinged, and he felt like a real cad.

"You're welcome," he said, his voice strangled. "I'll come by for you about seven-thirty."

"Fine," Milly agreed with a vague wave. When the door closed behind him, Milly allowed herself a wide grin. She headed back to bed. With any luck, by the time she got through with him tonight, Rolfe wouldn't know whether he was coming or going!

Part of Milly's strategy included wearing a "knock him dead" dress for Amalie's dinner party. Unfortunately, wrinkles didn't fit that image, so that afternoon, after making a remarkable recovery, thanks once again to her wacky metabolism, Milly went to borrow an iron from the Abington sisters. She strolled in through the rear door, only to come to an abrupt halt at the sound of raised voices coming from the parlor.

"Now, Miss Louella, you come to your senses!" said a strident male voice. "I'm offering you a fair price. If the bank forecloses on your mortgage, you'll have nothing to show for it!"

"Mr. Singleton, this house and our vineyards have been in the family for over eighty years. We have no intention of selling," said Louella Abington calmly.

Singleton! Milly recognized that name. She hurried into the parlor. First a defenseless puppy, and now two old women! How could any human stoop so low?

"Is something the matter, Louella?" Milly asked.

"Why, no, dear," Louella replied from her position on an ornately carved love seat. "I believe Mr. Singleton was just leaving." She stared haughtily down her aristocratic nose until Dean flushed to the top of his balding head. He began to gather his materials, flinging a leather-bound checkbook into his briefcase in a show of ill temper.

"You'll regret this, Miss Louella," he warned ominously. He glared at Milly, who stood her ground inside the doorway and barely resisted the urge to stick out her tongue at him.

"I'm certain that I shan't, Mr. Singleton," replied Louella. "A decision made in haste means that one must repent in leisure. You'll excuse us?" Louella ended coldly.

"Let me know when you change your mind," Dean snapped, his irritation at this summary dismissal evident in the curl of his lower lip. "But don't expect my offer to be as generous in the future." He grabbed the handle of his briefcase and stomped out of the room, slamming the front door behind him so hard the windowpanes rattled.

"Unpleasant person," Louella said with a sniff, then smiled at Milly. "Come sit down, dear. We'll all have tea to revive us after that ordeal."

"Lovely idea, Lulu," Florie agreed, calling her sister by her childhood name. "Milly has been so busy lately we haven't had time to visit. I'll just get it."

"I don't mean to pry, Louella," Milly said, "but are you in some kind of financial difficulty?"

"Heavens, child, this is nothing new." Louella laughed gently. "We'll get by. We always do," she said, dismissing the matter as Florie returned with the tea service.

Milly was very concerned about the Abington sisters' attitude toward their problems. Maybe they thought genteel ignorance would solve their difficulties, but Milly knew that most modern banks took a dim view of such a position. She tried to enjoy her tea, but the niggling worry made her uneasy for the women.

Later, borrowed iron in hand, Milly crossed the garden on her way back to her apartment. She paused, then walked over to where Buford was planting the last of the marigold seedlings.

"That looks nice," she said, admiring the yellow and orange blooms. Buford grunted in reply, then smoothed the soil one last time. Milly watched him thoughtfully. "Buford, did you know that Mr. Singleton just offered to buy this place?"

"It's not the first time that slick real estate feller's tried," Buford said, getting gingerly to his feet. He dusted the dirt from the knees of his old dungarees and chewed a little harder on his toothpick. "He's got some high-falutin' notion to make the place into a tourist attraction. He don't get nowhere, mostly."

"The ladies don't seem very concerned about their finances," Milly prompted.

Buford shrugged. "Things around here have been run down for the past twenty years. Without new equipment and a well-paid crew, it's hard to keep a vineyard productive."

"Are they in danger of losing their home?" Milly asked in alarm.

"Maybe, maybe not. They get by, but it's hard for them to understand business much, especially Miss Florie. She's just too much of a lady," Buford said.

Milly glanced at him sharply, struck by a sudden insight. Was Buford romantically attached to Florie? It didn't seem possible, looking at his weathered and wrinkled visage, but stranger things could happen. Milly smiled softly. Perhaps romance wasn't dead after all, at least not here in Altus.

81

"I wish there was some way to help them," she said, and Buford nodded sagely and agreed, but could offer no constructive suggestions.

Milly pondered the problem of the Abington sisters while she pressed her dress, but no solution came to her that would keep their pride intact. The two elderly women had become very dear to Milly in the short time she had known them. They had accepted her and taken her under their wing, and their acceptance touched the hidden core of Milly's heart that had been locked away since her mother's death.

Milly couldn't remember much about her mother, except that she was beautiful and always gay, but over the years whispered asides and subtle hints had revealed that too much money and too few responsibilities had led to her parents' early deaths. As a result, she had developed an aversion to the trappings of wealth. But at the moment she would glady have written out a check to ease the Abington sisters' burden. She sighed. She would have to keep working on this one.

When Rolfe knocked on the door promptly at seven-thirty, Milly gave herself one last satisfied glance in the mirror, then let him in. His reaction was all she could have wished for as he took in her appearance with a slightly glazed expression in his blue eyes.

Gone was Milly's usual casual attire, and in its place was a flame red dress of clingy silk that draped low in back and swirled in a circle about her slim legs when she walked. Sheer stockings and very high heels complimented the dress. Milly's hair framed her face in a mass of artful curls that begged a man's hands to crush them. Her makeup was a skillful blend of innocence and seduction, from the smoky shadow at her eyes to the carmine lip gloss that gleamed on her sensuous mouth.

"You look very nice," Rolfe choked out at last.

"Why, thank you, Rolfe," Milly said. "So do you." He wore the same suit he had worn in Hot Springs, and she was again struck by its conservative good taste and tailoring. She suppressed an inner sigh. Such a handsome man! Why couldn't things ever be simple? Despite a chemistry that could knock her socks off, they were so obviously wrong for each other in every other way. Rolfe couldn't understand her, and she knew she puzzled him most of the time and drove him crazy the rest of it. On the other hand, Rolfe couldn't seem to relax enough to have any fun, for he was often too serious. Still, maybe while she was in Altus she could get him to loosen up a little. A bit of teasing about their last encounter should rattle his innards, she decided with a hidden grin.

"Shall we go?" she suggested sweetly. They made the short trip to Amalie's in Rolfe's truck with little conversation. Rolfe said his mother had invited a few friends and neighbors over so that she could meet more people. Milly was pleasantly surprised when the first person she saw as she walked in was Ben Rollins.

"Well, if it isn't our newest resident dragon-slayer!" Ben said with a laugh when he saw her. He gave a low whistle of appreciation at her appearance. "Or maybe you're the princess! I'll never find out because my wife's the jealous type! Libby, come meet Milly," he said, drawing closer a petite woman whose short red curls bobbed over her friendly freckled face.

"Hi, Milly." Libby Rollins grinned. "And don't mind Ben. I'm not really jealous, because nobody in her right mind would have this man! Now, on the other hand, there's Rolfe, here . . ." She stretched up on tiptoe and pecked Rolfe on the cheek.

"I plead the fifth," Rolfe said, his blue eyes affectionate.

Amalie bustled over just then to greet Milly. "Don't you look wonderful!" she said. "Rolfe, get Milly a drink. We'll be starting dinner in just a little while."

Milly's eyes sparkled with mischief. "I'll have a little white wine, please," she said. "Perhaps some of that delightful Seyval Blanc?" She ignored Rolfe's frown, and when he hesitated, Ben said he'd be glad to get it and soon placed a slender stemmed goblet in Milly's hand.

"Are you sure you should drink that so soon after yesterday's, er—mishap?" Rolfe asked under his breath.

"Why, whatever do you mean?" Milly returned innocently, then turned away to meet some of Amalie's guests. She took a cautious sip just because she knew Rolfe was watching her like a hawk, but as she moved around the room she soon surreptitiously exchanged her nearly full glass for an empty one that had been left on a table. She was secretly amused at her little game and nearly laughed out loud when she saw the look of consternation on Rolfe's face as they all went in for supper.

The meal was a delight from beginning to end. Rolfe sat at the head of the table in Amalie's old-fashioned formal dining room, with Milly on his right while his mother took her place at the opposite end. A large arrangement of pink roses and candles graced the center of the table, and the atmosphere was relaxed and convivial, the conversation ranging through a myriad fascinating subjects.

Rolfe played the part of sommelier, opening a new bottle of a Hart Familie vintage for each successive course, but he always hesitated over Milly's glass, then filled it only half-full. As they worked their way through crabmeat appetizer, spinach salad and apricot-glazed cornish game hens, Rolfe's anxiety over

Milly's consumption of wine increased in proportion to the number of half-glasses that kept disappearing. He couldn't know that she adroitly emptied every glass into the centerpiece while his attention was elsewhere. Each time Rolfe looked up, her glass was empty again. By the time the frozen strawberry mousse was served, Rolfe was certain that there was going to be a repeat of the previous night's performance. Even though Milly seemed to be having a perfectly normal discussion with Ben, it was clear that another fiasco was just a matter of time.

"So you'll be able to print the auction catalog right here in Altus?" Milly asked Ben. She had just learned that he was publisher of the weekly newspaper, the Altus *Spectator,* and also did job printing.

"No problem," Ben assured her. "Just get me everything as soon as possible. We'll get it out for you before business picks up from the Grape Festival."

"Now don't get started on the Grape Festival!" Libby admonished from across the table.

"Ben is this year's chairman," Rolfe explained to Milly. His eyes narrowed as he studied her suspiciously.

"Yeah, and if I ever take it on again, remind me to kill myself first!" Ben grumbled.

"Oh, no, here it comes." Libby giggled.

"Woman! A little respect, please!" Ben said, his tone aggrieved. "For the last month I've been up to my eyeballs in arrangements for the darned thing! The scheduling is a nightmare! Arm wrestling and sack races, not to mention the tug-of-war contest! Pie-baking and grape-seed-spitting competitions. And I've still got to hire a band to play at the masked ball! Will your shed be available for that, Rolfe?"

"Sure." He nodded. "The auction will be over and things should be cleared away by then." Milly felt a little pang at the ease with which he said that, realizing that she would be gone by then, too. Well, she might as well have a little fun while she was here. She eased off her high-heeled shoe under the table.

"Well, I just hope I live through it!" Ben grumbled.

"Don't pay any attention," Rolfe advised Milly. "Ben forecasts disaster and then always produces great results."

"It sounds like fun," Milly said brightly.

Ben put on a morose expression. "Oh, yeah? Well, how would you like to organize our newest event—the snake rodeo?"

"What?" Milly's jaw dropped, and she wondered if her ears were deceiving her. Her bare foot halted in its stealthy path toward Rolfe as visions of snakes in tiny chaps and cowboy hats galloped through her mind.

"Whoever brings in the longest snake wins," Libby explained. She shuddered. "It's awful!"

"Isn't that rather dangerous?" Milly asked. "What if they get loose?"

She heard Rolfe's snort of disbelief. "Not live snakes! The longest dead one wins," Rolfe said, positive anew that her brain was wine-soaked.

"Ugh. That's a relief—I guess," she replied with a delicate shiver.

"Next to the dance, it'll probably be the best attended event," Ben said.

"Not by me!" Libby said.

"I think I'd have to pass on that one, too," Milly said and laughed.

"Well, we've got to do something to catch the public's attention," Ben said. "I wish I could think up a really different gimmick for publicity. There's got to be a way to bring those tourist dollars into Altus!"

"There's no reason to get ridiculous," Rolfe said gruffly. "I'd like to see us keep our dignity at least."

"Where's the fun in that?" Ben grinned.

"There's no reason to be a laughingstock, either," Rolfe retorted. "Remember the hot air balloon that wouldn't float? And the parade that got lost? Please, Ben, spare me and the rest of the town your hare-brained ideas!"

Milly was growing more and more irritated with Rolfe's pompous attitude. "I don't know," she said, letting her words slur slightly. She placed her chin in her palm and stared at Rolfe with a lazy, sultry look in her smoky green eyes. "Nothing ventured, nothing gained."

She stretched her bare foot out and ran her big toe down Rolfe's hard-muscled calf. She nearly laughed when she saw him jump. He tried to shift away, but she had already caught the edge of his pants leg with her toes and now massaged the curve of his calf through the material. She looked back at Ben as Rolfe's ears began to redden.

"I'm glad someone around here appreciates me!" Ben said.

"Oh, honey, I appreciate you!" Libby giggled.

Suddenly Rolfe's chair scraped back loudly and he stood, freeing himself from Milly's suggestive ministrations.

"Are you ready to serve coffee, Mother?" Rolfe asked, his voice thick.

Amalie broke off her conversation at the other end of the table and looked at her son in surprise. "Well, I suppose so," she answered. "Shall we take it in the living room, everyone?"

Rolfe stepped behind Milly's chair as she hastily shoved her foot into her shoe. She rose sedately as he helped her up.

"Thank you," she said, glancing up blandly into his enigmatic expression.

"The pleasure is all mine," he murmured, and his large warm hand gently pressed into her bare back. The gesture was perfectly innocuous to the casual observer, merely a gentleman's politeness, yet Milly felt the subtle persuasion of his strong fingers against her sensitive skin. Her temperature immediately began to rise, and she moved fractionally away from him, hoping the telltale warmth would not stain her cheeks. It occurred to her that she was playing with fire when she teased Rolfe.

Seated on the sofa a few moments later, Milly was further disconcerted when Rolfe sat beside her and placed a cup of black coffee in her hands.

"Drink," he said sternly. Milly raised the cup to her lips to cover their sudden quivering. Rolfe watched her closely, his mouth a straight line and his expression assessing, as Milly strove to remain calm. She sipped the brew and did her best to follow the conversation going on around them, but it was hard to do so when Rolfe's lean hip was pressed close to hers and his arm lay relaxed behind her shoulders on the sofa back. His nearness was unnerving.

"Aren't you finished harvesting, Rolfe?" Ben asked then.

Rolfe nodded, but his intent gaze never left Milly's face. "Uh-huh. Just another week or so to finish the cleanup," he said.

"Oh, great!" Libby bubbled. "Then everything will work out perfectly!"

Rolfe frowned and looked at Libby. "What everything?" he asked.

"You haven't forgotten about our canoe trip, have you?" Libby asked.

"I have to admit I'd forgotten all about it, Lib," Rolfe replied with an apologetic grimace. Milly was grateful that his attention had shifted away from her.

She had been finding it increasingly difficult to breathe.

"We're counting on your being there," Libby told him.

"Don't worry, I wouldn't miss it for the world," Rolfe assured her. Milly could see that Rolfe valued his easy friendship with Ben and Libby. The give and take proved their relationship must be a solid one of long standing, and Milly was a bit envious. Why couldn't Rolfe be as open with her? She sipped the coffee and tried not to feel depressed.

"How about it, Milly?" Ben asked. "Don't you want to come, too?"

"We float trip on the White River," Libby explained. "You should do it while you're here. You'll never see such beautiful scenery."

"I'm not sure Milly should attempt such an expedition," Rolfe interjected. "I don't imagine she's had much experience with that sort of thing."

"I've been canoeing before!" Milly said belligerently. Her small chin jutted forward in a stubborn line. She was getting sick and tired of Rolfe trying to tell her what to do! His tendency to be overprotective was nearly smothering her. No one need know the only time she'd been in a canoe was at a museum exhibit. What could be hard about holding a paddle? "I'd like very much to go," she said in defiance.

"Great! You'll love it!" Ben said heartily, and immediately plunged into plans for the coming trip.

Rolfe leaned over and murmured in Milly's ear. "Are you going to remember all these wild plans tomorrow?"

"What plans?" she asked mischievously.

Rolfe's mouth twisted in a reluctant smile. "You're headed for trouble, lady," he said softly, his blue eyes smoldering. Milly swallowed and glanced away as her heart drummed into double time. It looked as though her plans to rattle him were definitely backfiring!

She stood up suddenly. "I need some air," she said raggedly. She was dismayed when Rolfe rose, too.

"That's a good idea. Let's tell Mother good night," he said. As they made their departure, Libby promised to telephone Milly later in the week with details about the canoe trip. Within minutes they were in the truck again. Milly decided to play it safe. It might be cowardly, but she rested her head on the seat back and feigned inebriated exhaustion.

Rolfe drove in silence, and Milly risked a glance. She sat up suddenly.

"Where are we going?" she demanded. This was not the familiar road to the Abington house.

"I want to show you something," Rolfe replied, looking straight ahead.

"Really, Rolfe," Milly said with a laugh shaky from apprehension, "I'm very tired. I—I think I've had too much to drink again."

"You're as sober as a judge." He said the words with such absolute conviction that Milly knew there was no point in trying to refute his statement. She merely stared as he loosened his tie and pulled it free of his shirt collar, then flung it up on the dash. Was it her imagination, or was his manner subtly menacing? What kind of retribution was in store for her because of the game she had played under the table? Rolfe shifted the truck gears, then pulled in onto the shoulder of the road and parked. He gestured out the windshield. "What do you think?"

Milly glanced ahead and then breathed in a surprised gasp of pleasure at the scene laid out below them. They were parked on the curve of the road overlooking the Altus valley. A huge summer moon hung low on the horizon, bathing the scene with silver.

"How beautiful!" She felt the warmth of Rolfe's hand lightly caressing the side of her neck. Turning, she saw that he was looking at her intently.

"My words exactly," he murmured, and she knew he was not referring to the scenery. She flushed hotly and pulled away from his touch, although it hurt her to do so.

"I'll bet you used to bring all your girlfriends up here when you were in school," she said, laughing nervously.

She saw the white gleam of Rolfe's teeth. "It's been known to happen on occasion," he said. "Right now I'm having a hard time remembering. Seems there's a lot of that going around."

Milly gave him a startled look, then quickly glanced away. "Oh?"

"For example, just what do you recall about last night?" he asked. He swiftly caught her arms and pulled her toward him.

Milly's hands rested against his white shirt, and she gave an uneasy laugh. "Really, Rolfe, all that wine—"

"Maybe you need a gentle reminder," he interrupted. His mouth covered hers before she could protest, and he kissed her thoroughly and with excruciating tenderness. When he lifted his head, she gasped for breath and her heart pounded in her ears. "Remember anything yet?"

Milly shook her head, not trusting herself to speak.

"This lapse of memory is harder to overcome than I thought," Rolfe muttered, then caught her chin and kissed her again, his mouth like warm velvet. Silver tingles shot down Milly's nerve endings, sparkling in the darkness behind her eyes and fraying the silken cord of her composure. "Nothing yet?" he asked finally, his voice husky.

"I—I'm beginning to recall a few details," Milly managed hoarsely.

"We'll keep trying if it takes all night," he promised and bent toward her once more.

Milly began to feel a bit panicky. Rolfe's attentions were having their usual effect on her and in a few more seconds she wouldn't care about anything! She placed a resisting hand against his chest.

"Really, Rolfe!" she gasped. "You know your kisses are too spectacular to forget."

A devilish grin appeared on his face. "Thought so."

"Oh, you arrogant man! You knew all the time!" she accused. She pushed against him, but he held her securely in the circle of his arms.

"Not all the time," he admitted. His expression became suddenly serious. "Honesty is important to me, Milly."

"I—I didn't mean to make you angry," she said falteringly, inwardly cringing at the ominous sound of his words. If he felt this strongly about a little joke, what would he do if he ever learned she had been hiding her true circumstances? Would it appear that she had come to them under false pretenses?

"And that crack about taking advantage of you," Rolfe continued. "That was a low blow."

"I was just teasing you," Milly protested. "Pretend you have a sense of humor for once! You certainly deserved everything you got for giving me such a hangover!"

"Teasing? I nearly jumped out of my skin when your foot touched mine under the dinner table. It would have really shocked my mother if she could have read my mind just then." Milly blushed at his words. "By the way, what did you do with all the wine you supposedly drank tonight?" he asked as an afterthought.

"Your mother's roses are now pickled pink," she explained wryly.

"You didn't!" He groaned. She nodded solemnly. "My wonderful wine wasted!"

"But those roses are happy!" she said with a laugh. She felt Rolfe's chest move with a deep rumble of laughter. Milly relaxed against him and enjoyed the warm, protected feeling of his embrace.

Rolfe inhaled her scent. "You always smell good," he murmured. "Such a sweet fragrance that's uniquely yours. I swear I could pick you out of a crowd blindfolded." His hand slipped beneath the drape of her dress at her back and traced the outline of her spine.

"Don't, Rolfe," she whispered.

"Give me a couple of good reasons why not," he murmured against her neck. His breath stirred a frisson of chill-bumps along her skin, but Milly's brain was in confusion. No matter how much she longed to remain in his arms, there was already too much between them.

"I drive you crazy." She felt his chest move again with muffled laughter.

"In more ways than one," he admitted. His lips moved across her bare shoulder, and Milly struggled to control her breathing.

"I'm not tipsy, either," she said. Her eyes fluttered closed as a melting lethargy sapped her strength.

"I promised you wouldn't be," he said agreeably.

His complacent words jolted Milly out of her stupor, and she jerked upright. "Please, Rolfe! For once in my life I'm trying not to be headstrong and impulsive, but you're making it extremely difficult!" She struggled for the right words. "I'll be out of your life soon. It would be better if I left with no regrets."

Rolfe eased his hold on her, and she tilted her chin

so she could read his expression. An eyebrow arched in a sardonic question mark, and his lips twisted.

"That's just about how my luck runs." He sighed in resignation. "Don't you ever get tired of wandering?"

"It's part of my job," she said with a tiny shrug. "Besides, there's no one to go home to anymore." There was a poignant, lonely note in her husky voice that caught at Rolfe's heart. Milly's emerald eyes were filled with turbulent emotions. "Things are happening too fast. You understand, don't you?"

Rolfe drew another deep breath. "I understand, and in saner moments I'm sure I would agree, but that doesn't make it any easier, does it?"

Milly bit her lip as their eyes met, and they studied each other gravely. "No," she said at last, acknowledging aloud what had been unspoken between them. Her voice was barely a whisper. "It makes it harder."

CHAPTER SIX

Milly was too busy over the next couple of weeks to brood over Rolfe Hart. At least that's what she tried to tell herself as she tackled the jobs at hand, but there was always a tight knot in the vicinity of her heart when she thought of him. A thousand times a day she found herself listening for the sound of his voice, but the only thing conspicuous about Rolfe was his absence.

Since the night of Amalie's dinner party, she and Rolfe had lived under a truce that consisted of a full retreat. Neither one of them was willing to risk going any further in their uneven relationship, and so they were stalemated. They saw as little of each other as possible, and when they were forced together by circumstances, they were polite but nothing more. Surely this strategy was a cure for heart-foolishness. Why, then, did the man continue to preoccupy Milly to the point of absentminded distraction?

Milly slapped the stapler against another catalog and took a look around Amalie's cluttered living room. Card tables groaned under the weight of flyers and finished catalogs. Amalie typed address labels, which Louella then neatly applied to a pile of completed books. Florie and Libby Rollins assembled catalog pages by walking around another table, then handed the completed book to Milly for stapling.

"We're nearly done," Libby announced.

"Wonderful!" Milly said, thumping the stapler yet again. "This isn't tiring you out too much, is it, Florie?"

"Good gracious, no! I haven't had so much fun since St. Mary's last bingo tournament!" Florie answered.

"I must admit, I'll be glad when we're done," Louella added, "but it's hard to believe how much we've accomplished today."

"Last address!" Amalie said, ripping the sheet of labels from the typewriter. The group gave a ragged cheer.

"You ladies have been wonderful," Milly said. "We'll get this in the mail today. Then we can all sit back and relax until auction day."

"Ready for our canoe trip, Milly?" Libby asked.

"Sure. It'll be a perfect get-away-from-it-all the day before the auction," Milly agreed. "Just the thing to take my mind off it."

"We're so lucky to have you organize all this for us," Amalie said. She began pasting on labels with Louella, and Milly redoubled her stapling speed.

"I think we've covered everything," Milly said. "Ads are scheduled to run in the Fort Smith and Little Rock papers, and I've arranged for a portable sign the day of the auction."

"And Ben will put an article in the *Spectator* every week until then," Libby promised, handing Milly another completed catalog.

"The price he gave the historical society for printing was a bargain, too," Milly said. "Be sure and thank him again—and thank you, Libby, for pitching in."

"Glad to help. I'll admit that I sometimes get bored over the summer. I can't wait to get back to my high school students in the fall."

"I can't believe you can control a pack of wild kids," Milly said, grinning at Libby, who looked as young as her students in a loose pullover and jeans.

"I'm a powerhouse," Libby said, showing her freckled biceps in an imitation of a bodybuilder.

"Did you go to school in Little Rock, dear?" Amalie asked Milly.

"I attended boarding school in the East, then my guardian sent me to Europe for finishing school before college," Milly explained.

"Great-aunt Lavinia attended a Swiss finishing school," offered Florie.

"No, that had to be Cousin-once-removed Sophie," Louella argued gently.

"Now, Lulu, I'm almost positive . . ." The elderly women wrangled good-naturedly in the background as Amalie continued thoughtfully.

"You know, Rolfe spent a year in France studying with a master vintner. You and he have a lot in common."

Milly made a noncommittal murmur and hastily began stacking addressed and stamped catalogs in a box to be taken to the post office.

"And you almost had a French daughter-in-law," Libby reminded Amalie. "Whatever happened to her?"

"You mean Monique?" Amalie gave a dainty shrug. "That engagement was an unfortunate mistake. It's just as well it didn't work out, but it changed Rolfe. I missed him terribly that year," Amalie confided. Her eyes, so like her son's, clouded at the memory. She gave her silver and gold curls a shake and smiled at Milly. "I'm sure that it was equally hard to leave your family."

"My parents were killed when I was young, and Cousin Howard was relieved to have me out from un-

97

der his feet," Milly said. Her brain was reeling at the picture of Rolfe engaged to a glamorous French-woman, but her unselfconscious admission made Amalie frown. There was a matching frown on Rolfe's face as he stood at the door surveying the chaos of the living room.

"Hi, Rolfe!" Libby piped as she spotted him. "Want to help?"

"Looks as though you've got it under control," Rolfe said, coming forward. He didn't want to feel any sympathy for Milly's lonely childhood; neither did he want to feel guilty about his own happy upbringing. It didn't matter. He felt both and was unreasonably irritated. But then he had been irritated about a great number of things since Milly had come into his life, mainly his inability to resolve just where she fit into it. It didn't help his mood that she hadn't even looked up when he walked in and seemed intent on ignoring him.

"I've got something for Milly," he said.

Milly gave a little start and looked up. She hastily thrust the remainder of the catalogs into the box and dusted off her hands. She gave Rolfe a shy, tentative smile that caught the attention of the four other females in the room. Louella gave a sage little nod, and the other three silently agreed. There was something going on between those two, something special. The delighted women settled back to watch.

"What have you got for me?" Milly asked. Her eyes widened as Rolfe held out a key ring. "My jeep? You've brought my jeep?"

"Right outside," Rolfe said.

Milly gave a whoop and snatched the keys out of Rolfe's hand, then flung her arms around his neck and gave him a resounding kiss. She flew out the door, her cheeks burning. Rolfe rubbed his chin and tried not to look nonplussed while the women hid their smiles.

"Do you think Milly missed her jeep?" Libby finally asked, then dissolved into giggles.

Before Rolfe could frame a reply, his mother had pushed the box of catalogs into his arms. "Why don't you take this out to her?" she suggested.

Rolfe was happy to make his escape. He felt the tips of his ears reddening under the Abington sisters' covert scrutiny and knew that his mother's bland expression hid her approval. He groaned inwardly. The next thing he knew, the whole town would be matchmaking!

Outside, he found Milly making a minute inspection of her jeep. She looked up at him with amazement written all over her face.

"Rolfe! All you had to do was fix the taillight!" she said. "What did you do to it?" Rolfe set the box of catalogs in the backseat and shuffled his feet uncomfortably.

"Now, don't fly off the handle, Milly," he warned. "One thing led to another. They had to repaint it because no other paint would match, then the engine needed tuning, so—"

"It's beautiful! But I can't let you pay for all this!"

Rolfe gave a sigh of relief that she approved of the changes. "My insurance took care of it," he said negligently. It hadn't, but he'd never tell her that. It was a relief to him that she had a vehicle she could trust.

"Insurance paid all of it?" she asked suspiciously. Her eyes scanned the shiny candy apple red coat of paint and the sparkling chrome. Why, her jeep hadn't even been this *clean* since she bought it! Suddenly a lump grew in her throat and tears welled in her eyes. She knew that this was Rolfe's way of giving her something. He might never send her roses or heart-shaped boxes of candy, but this gesture showed he cared about her.

"Thank you," she said huskily.

"You're not crying?" He was thunderstruck. Milly laughed at his expression and dashed the tears away with the back of her hand.

"No, I'm not crying!" She caught his hand and pulled him into the jeep. "Come on, I'll take you for a ride!"

Milly insisted they stop at her apartment to pick up Sebastian for the ride. Then they made a flying tour of Altus and vicinity, stopping once to drop off the catalogs at the post office.

Milly was exhilarated and laughing with pleasure at the return of her jeep, and although her driving reduced Rolfe to a white-knuckled state of quivering anxiety, he had to admit that she was able to experience a rare kind of joy in even the simplest things. He sat back, idly stroking Sebastian's furry ears, and watched as the fresh summer breeze blew the dark tendrils of hair back from Milly's shining countenance. She was so open, so transparent in her feelings, and even her looniest actions were seasoned by an inner sweetness. She couldn't help it if this sometimes led her into trouble, Rolfe acknowledged as Milly glanced at him, her smile radiant. It was her nature to meet life head on, and Rolfe felt a prick of envy when he compared his overly cautious personality to Milly's. Who was really getting more enjoyment out of life?

"Thanks for the ride," he said when Milly dropped him off at the winery.

"Thank you, Rolfe! I'm glad to have my wheels back! Isn't that so, Sebastian?" she crooned, scratching the pup's chest until his leg thumped in doggy ecstasy. Rolfe laughed.

"You'll spoil him," he warned.

"I don't care. He's the only pet I've ever had, and I'm trying to make up for lost time," Milly said.

"You mean you never had any kind of pet before?" Rolfe asked in amazement and sudden sympathy. He thought briefly of the succession of dogs, cats, and assorted reptiles that had populated his childhood.

"Nope. It wasn't feasible while I was off at school," Milly explained. "How big do you think he'll get?"

"Hard to say with a mixed breed," Rolfe replied. His large hands examined Sebastian. "But with the size of these paws, I hope you have stock in a dog food company!"

Milly laughed, inwardly amused because she was sure she did somewhere in her portfolio of investments. "Oh, well, I'm going to keep him anyway," she said lovingly. Rolfe was struck by the unplumbed depths of her affection. What would it be like to be the human object of that love? The thought was somehow utterly attractive.

He watched Milly drive away with a perplexed expression on his face. Did he have the courage to risk his orderly existence for what he thought he saw in Milly?

After that day it was a common sight to see Milly buzzing around Atlus in her bright red jeep. The townspeople invariably waved and smiled when they saw the pretty girl driving such an unlikely vehicle, sometimes with Louella or Florie beside her, and always with Sebastian hanging over the backseat, his long ears flapping in the wind.

Louella and Milly spent a lot of time investigating old cemeteries in the area for information to add to the genealogy and history Louella had been compiling over the years. Her work progressed slowly, she told Milly, mainly due to the difficulty involved in her visiting the research facilities at the University of Arkansas at Fayetteville. Because of the distance, she couldn't go nearly as often as she would have liked, so Milly started teaching Louella to drive the jeep.

"She's eighty if she's a day," Rolfe had upbraided Milly after he saw the driving lesson. "What on earth were you thinking about?"

"She's spry and has wonderful coordination, and besides that, she enjoys it!" Milly retorted heatedly. "It gives her a sense of freedom! Since when are you so prejudiced against the elderly?"

"Prejudiced!" Rolfe left abruptly, feeling beaten, and whenever he saw Louella in the jeep after that he would close his eyes and pray.

Milly was up at dawn the Saturday of the canoe trip. She had worked hard all week, and everything was ready for tomorrow's auction. All the items were tagged and numbered; chairs, sound equipment, and podium were in place, and now all there was left to do was pray for good weather for Sunday afternoon. And if it was anything like today's beautiful conditions, everything would be fine.

Milly wore a pink bikini under her matching T-shirt and shorts. Her hair was pulled back in a ponytail, and she carried a visor and a tote bag with a change of clothes, towel, and suntan lotion. The sun was barely peeping over the horizon when Ben honked for her, and she joined Ben and Libby in their long white station wagon. Rolfe was already there, as well as the Henrys, a couple that Milly remembered from Amalie's party.

Conversation was desultory and drowsy as they made the hour-and-a-half drive north to the shores of Beaver Lake near Eureka Springs. Rolfe explained that for float trips it was more convenient to rent canoes from a concessionaire, who would take you to a

102

starting point, then pick you up at a designated spot downstream and return you to your car at the end of the day.

Milly felt her excitement growing as they reached their destination and rented the canoes. There was an unspoken agreement that she and Rolfe would share a canoe, so she helped him load the waterproof bundles of equipment into the aluminum canoe. She couldn't help but notice how super he looked in his cutoffs, his bare legs long and tanned and lightly sprinkled with golden hair.

Rolfe caught her a few minutes later looking with some trepidation at their wobbling craft. Somehow the canoe she had seen at the museum exhibit hadn't seemed quite so large or unstable. Of course, it had been an Indian canoe of birch bark, and this one was shiny aluminum with a jaunty red strip down its side.

"Something the matter?" he asked.

"Oh, no, of course not," Milly returned. She buckled the last strap on her mandatory orange life jacket. "It's just that I didn't remember a canoe being so long. Shall I get in now?"

"Go ahead," he said. Milly gingerly stepped into the canoe and felt it rasp gently against the gravel in the shallows along the river's edge. Here the water was wide and flat and smooth, the current hardly evident. She sat down in the prow, grasped her paddle, and shrugged away her foolish nervousness. This wasn't going to be hard at all.

"Everybody ready?" Ben asked. "Then let's go. Stay together and we'll break about noon to eat the lunch Libby packed."

Milly gave a little gasp and lurched as Rolfe pushed them free of the shore, then nimbly hopped into the canoe, the water squishing in his worn canvas sneakers.

"Just head downstream," he said, dipping his paddle with obvious skill. "We really don't have to do much work other than keep ourselves pointed in the right direction."

"Like this?" Milly asked, jabbing her paddle awkwardly into the water and immediately slanting the canoe sideways against the current. Rolfe hastily adjusted his stroke until they were headed correctly downstream again.

"Not quite," he said with a groan. "You did say you'd been canoeing before, didn't you?"

"Well, it has been a while," Milly said, casting an anxious glance back over her shoulder at Rolfe.

"Mil-ly." Rolfe's tone said he wasn't buying her story at all.

"All right, so I've never actually been in the water before," she admitted. "Just tell me what to do."

Rolfe groaned again. "Don't do anything!" he ordered. "You just enjoy the ride and let me do the paddling and steering. We'll both be a lot safer—and drier —that way!"

"You don't have to treat me like a total imbecile!" Milly cried in annoyance. "I can help paddle! Whoops!" Her violent movement as she turned to glare at Rolfe sent the canoe rocking from side to side. She dropped her paddle into the bottom of the canoe and hung on for dear life.

"You two okay?" Ben called across the water.

"Just making a few, er—adjustments," Rolfe answered. He stroked strongly into the water and sent the canoe scudding ahead as he glowered at Milly. "If you keep going at this rate, we're not going to make it past the first bend in the river, much less the white water. And I'm going to be too tired to paddle!"

"I'm sorry," Milly murmured, much subdued.

Rolfe relented at her woebegone expression and

gave a sigh. "Look, do it like this," he instructed, and her face immediately brightened. "But easily! Don't do anything I can't fix!"

"Okay, I'll really try," she promised. And she did. For the next few hours Milly enjoyed the delights of the natural wonders along the White River. Her meager attempts to help Rolfe with the paddling made her feel as though she were pulling her own weight, and they got along comfortably.

The cool of the early morning quickly evaporated as the sun rose higher in the sky, but the river was shadowed in many places by bluffs covered with the thick evergreen branches of tall cedars. The river narrowed in these places and the current flowed faster, a silent and tireless companion. Milly knew she had never seen anything more beautiful. Occasionally a rainbow trout would jump in the clear water. Rolfe pointed out ospreys, jays, and a stately great blue heron, his fringed crest as kingly as any crown as he stood on one leg in the shallows.

Milly was content to absorb the majestic loveliness in silence. When the river again widened, they guided their canoes to a flat gravel beach, then went ashore to have lunch with the others.

They stuffed themselves with Libby's fried chicken and potato salad, deviled eggs, and brownies, washed down with canned drinks cooled in the near-frigid water of the river. Afterward the warm sun and their full stomachs made everyone drowsy. Libby lay with her head in Ben's lap, while the Henrys explored the bank and Milly tried her hand at skimming stones. Rolfe had produced a fly rod and was upstream practicing his casting.

"I don't know what's the matter with me these days," Libby murmured, stifling a yawn. "Can't seem to catch up on my sleep."

"If you don't mind," Mike Henry said, "Jan and I will go on ahead. There's a tributary I've been wanting to explore."

"Sure," Ben said, giving a slow wave. "We'll be down after Libby's siesta." Libby was sound asleep, curled into a ball like a child.

After a while Rolfe returned from upstream. "No luck?" Ben asked.

"Not a bite," Rolfe replied in disgust.

"Why don't you and Milly go on so you can do a little fishing?" Ben suggested. "We'll catch up later."

"You don't mind?" Rolfe asked.

"Go ahead. I've a mind to catch a little shut-eye, too," Ben said and lay back, tipping his battered hat over his eyes.

"That suit you, Milly?" Milly dropped her collection of water-smoothed stones and nodded. "Put on your life jacket, then."

"Do I have to?" Milly protested. "It's so hot."

"Yes, you have to," Rolfe said, slipping into his own.

Reluctantly Milly did likewise. It was tiresome of Rolfe to be so by-the-book all the time!

Soon they were slowly moving downstream again. The brilliant afternoon sun dappled the water with spangles of light. Milly put on her visor and rubbed more sun screen into her exposed skin. Rolfe clamped his jaw shut grimly at the sight of her hands moving over the soft skin of her inner thighs and resolutely cast his line, although fishing was the furthest thing from his mind. An occasional dip of his paddle kept them on course as the river began to pick up speed again.

"Ah! Got you!" This muffled utterance and the whirr of Rolfe's reel caused Milly to rouse from her sunbathing just in time to see him pull a wriggling silver-scaled fish into the canoe.

"You caught one!" she said, delighted.

Rolfe grinned, his teeth white in his tanned face. He deftly removed the hook and held up the fish by its mouth for her inspection.

"He's a beauty, isn't he?" he said. "That's a rainbow trout."

"Gorgeous!" Milly watched in surprise as Rolfe gently slipped the fish back into the river. "Why didn't you keep him?"

"I haven't caught enough to eat, and I don't want a trophy. Let someone else have the sport of catching that one again," he said, shrugging.

Milly was impressed in spite of herself. A man with a feeling for nature like that couldn't be all bad.

"Do you think I could try?" she asked diffidently. A hesitant look crossed Rolfe's face, then he nodded.

"Sure, what harm could you do?" This wasn't exactly the reaction Milly wanted, but the results were the same. Rolfe checked to see that the fly with its dangerously barbed hooks was still secure, then passed the rod to Milly.

Milly sat up straight and admired the shiny gadget. Now, let's see, she mused, Rolfe draws it back and—

"Ow! Watch it!" Rolfe shouted, batting the fly away from his face.

"Oops, sorry!" Milly bit her lip and tried again, this time managing to send the bait in a credible arc to land with a plop in the water. "What do I do if I get a bite?" she asked.

"Just turn the little crank to reel him in," Rolfe explained. He was captivated by the look of shining pleasure on Milly's face. Her nose was sunburned, her hair was falling down out of its ponytail, but she had never looked more beautiful. It was hard not to reach out and hold her right there in the middle of the river.

They traveled a bit like this, Milly casting the line, Rolfe offering tips and suggestions, until the eddies of the increasing current caused the canoe to pick up speed. Looking ahead, Rolfe could see the beginnings of the white foam that marked the shallow rapids that were the high point of a float trip on this portion of the White.

"Better reel it in," he advised, grasping his paddle more securely. "We're getting close to the white water."

"White water?" Milly gasped. She looked up in sudden horror and saw the approaching rapids. "You don't mean we're going through *that?*"

"Relax, it's nothing to worry about," Rolfe began, but his words were broken off at Milly's scream. "What is it? Don't be afraid—"

"I got one!" Milly hollered, slinging the fishing rod from side to side. "I caught a fish!"

"Well, reel it in!" Rolfe shouted over the increasing roar of the water. "No, don't stand up!"

But it was too late. In her excited attempt to drag in the fish, Milly stood, then fell backward out of the canoe. Too late, Rolfe reached for her, then hung suspended before he, too, was flung from the boat into the whirling, sucking grasp of the white water rapids.

Rolfe instinctively rolled into a ball to offer the least resistance, then bobbed to the surface, blinded by spray and foam. The relentless force of the surging water pushed him down the bobsled run of rapids, tossing him high, then flinging him low as if he were no more than a bit of flotsam. Fear for Milly held his heart in its chilly embrace. He couldn't see her, couldn't hear her over the pounding roar of the water. Rolfe gasped for breath, his hands flailing as he struggled to control his passage at breakneck speed down the steps. Agony cut through him. Had Milly made it this far?

Rolfe struggled to his feet in the waist-deep pool that spread out from the bottom of the rapids. He forced his shaking knees to support him as he wiped the water from his eyes. Suddenly his breath caught in his throat, and he began to thrash toward the orange life jacket floating on the other side of the pool. His hands were trembling as he reached for Milly.

Milly found her feet and stood up just as Rolfe reached her. She drew in great, gasping breaths, sputtering incoherently. Rolfe's hands were hard on her battered shoulders.

"My God, Milly! Are you all right?" he demanded, his voice cracking.

"That was—that was—" She gasped, then opened her eyes and blinked at Rolfe's pasty complexion. "The most—wonderful—exhilarating—"

"What? You could have been killed!" Rolfe yelled.

"Oh, no! It was great!" she stated, panting. Her mouth formed an audacious Cheshire-cat grin. "Could we do it again?"

Rolfe stared at her, his jaw hanging. His stomach was where his heart should have been, as though an elevator had dropped from beneath his feet without warning. Wouldn't he ever learn? Milly would never react to *anything* the way he expected.

He shook his head, suddenly laughing helplessly. Milly grinned, then joined in his mirth. Rolfe threw an arm around Milly's shoulders, and they splashed toward the shore. He was laughing so hard he had to hold his sides, and tears ran from the corners of his eyes down his drenched face.

"Rolfe?" Milly's expression was puzzled, then concerned. Rolfe's wheezing laughter unnerved her.

She fumbled with the clumsy buckles of her life vest, then tore at Rolfe's, pulling it free. He just laughed harder. For the first time since she had tumbled from the canoe, she was frightened.

My God, she thought, he's hysterical! She did the only thing she could think of. She slapped him.

For a stunned moment Rolfe was silenced. He raised a wondering hand to his cheek. "Do you really think that was necessary?" he asked, then began to chuckle again.

"Oh, stop, please, Rolfe," Milly begged, throwing herself against him and burying her face in the sodden fabric of his shirt.

"So you want to do it again?" Rolfe managed, gasping on a laugh. "Look at that," he said, pointing. "Do you think we should try it?"

Milly looked to where he was pointing and gasped. What was left of their canoe, its bottom ripped open, hung upside-down between two rocks at the bottom of the rapids.

"I—I—" She shuddered and buried her face against his chest once more, shaking her head mutely. Her hands tightened on him as his mirth subsided. "Hold me."

"Hey, it's all right," he soothed her huskily.

Rolfe's strong arms clenched tightly around her in a sudden spasm, and he rested his cheek on the top of her head. They held each other for a long moment.

"Come on, let's get higher up on the bank. We'll have to flag down Ben and Libby when they come through."

"Wait, there's some of our gear," Milly said. She went down to the edge of the water and retrieved a paddle and her soaked tote bag, then came back to Rolfe. "I didn't see anything else."

"It doesn't matter." He stuck the paddle into the

gravel and draped their life jackets over it as a kind of signal flag. Then he led Milly up the bank and helped her over the edge of the low bluff. The grass was thick and soft, and a stunted tree provided fitful shade in the late afternoon sunlight. A soft breeze rustled the leaves, causing Milly to shiver in her damp clothes, sick at heart and full of self-reproach.

"You're cold." Rolfe sat down next to her on the grass.

"I'm all right."

"Take off your wet things. They'll dry in no time." He pulled off his own wet shirt and unsnapped his cutoffs, sliding out of them to reveal a narrow Olympic-style bathing suit. When Milly made no move to follow his suggestion, he sighed. "Come on, Milly. You'll be more comfortable."

His hands tugged impersonally at her drenched T-shirt, peeling it off her body and over her head. He spread their clothes on the grass, then turned back to Milly, but his breath caught and his blue eyes widened at the sight of her. Her full breasts heaved against the narrow band of her bikini top, and her eyes were wide and emerald green and swimming with unshed tears.

"Now what is it?" he asked.

With a sob Milly flung her arms around him and buried her face against his neck.

"Oh, Rolfe, I'm so sorry," she said through her sobs. "I wrecked the canoe, and lost your fishing rod, and scared us both to death." Rolfe looked down helplessly at the slim woman in his arms, then gathered her closer.

"Hush, honey, don't cry," he murmured against her hair, now drying in wisps and tendrils in the warm summer air. "It's all right."

"I'll pay for everything, I swear," she promised.

111

"I'll buy you a new fishing rod. Oh, you must *hate* me!"

"Oh, God, no. I don't hate you," he muttered. He gently pushed her onto her back and stared deeply into her tear-drenched eyes. He lowered his head just as she reached for him, and their kiss seemed to go on forever.

Milly savored the texture of Rolfe's kiss, and she clung to him, melting like honey against the warmth of his chest. Her fingers moved restlessly through the soft thickness of his hair, teased the curls at his nape, then stroked the hard tendons in his neck.

With a groan Rolfe released her lips, then kissed her eyes, her chin, and the long graceful column of her neck as Milly arched against him.

"Oh, God. I want to touch every inch of you," he murmured. His tongue flicked across her delicate collarbone as his hands roamed along the indentations of her waist, pushing down her damp shorts and tossing them aside. His fingers were sensually tender as they moved along her thighs, and Milly murmured incoherently at the pleasure. "When I think how close I came to losing you . . ." His voice trailed off as his hands massaged the rounded globes of her breasts.

Her mind was in chaos, every thought tumbled on the shoals of this lightning plunge into passion. From somewhere far away an inner voice urged her to be sensible, to *think* before she reacted to the devastating rapture of Rolfe's skilled caresses. Her hands captured his as they cupped her breasts.

"Wait, Rolfe," she begged. "What if they come . . ."

Her voice trailed off at the burning light behind his eyes. Her flesh quivered beneath his touch. There was something so incredibly sensual about sensing the pleasure he felt in touching her, his hands gently squeezing the swollen mounds while her hands rested on his, following the movements. His pleasure, her pleasure—it was a circle, going round and round until she couldn't tell where it began or where it would end.

Rolfe's fingers, twined in hers, slipped under the edge of the bikini top and pressed against her nipples. Milly gasped, her core melting into a molten center of longing at the erotic novelty of touching herself through him. Overcome, she freed her fingers, curling them up the hard wall of his chest.

She was rewarded by a low hungry growl, then Rolfe took her mouth again in an insatiable feast of lips and tongue. There was a wildness beating within her, made all the more pungent by the danger of discovery, the thrill of a forbidden fantasy. Rolfe tugged on the string of her bikini, at last releasing her bosom to his heated gaze.

"You are so beautiful," he breathed. His lips moved over the sweet flesh, then caught and gently tugged her turgid nipple. Milly moaned, her hands catching in his hair to press him even closer.

"Rolfe," she gasped, wanting him, his strong body, his sensitive heart, all of him. His mouth moved to her other breast, and Milly writhed under the waves of pleasure. Even her ride down the rapids hadn't been as thrilling as this. His large hands slipped under the band of her bikini bottoms to cup her buttocks, lifting her slightly to seat her fully against the swollen evidence of his manhood.

Milly gulped, tightening her arms about his neck as his lips found hers in a searing kiss of mutual desire. Suddenly she sensed a tense awareness in him. He lifted his head, listening, then groaned and rolled off onto his back, his elbow crooked over his eyes.

"Oh God," he said weakly. "Remind me to discuss timing with my friends."

"What?" His sudden, inexplicable withdrawal had left her reeling.

"We're being rescued, my dear."

CHAPTER SEVEN

Rolfe stood up and waved his shirt over his head, answering Ben's and Libby's anxious shouts. Milly pulled on her damp shirt and gathered the scattered articles of clothing. Her brain felt numb. She moved to the edge of the bluff, and Rolfe placed a supporting hand on her arm as they clambered over the edge. He held her firmly until she found her footing, then looked deeply into her eyes.

"We have unfinished business, you and I," he said, his voice husky and his eyes a stormy blue. He tucked a strand of hair behind her ear as she gazed at him, her silence a testimony to the turbulence of her emotions. Then he led her down to the water's edge, where Ben and Libby waited with concerned faces.

"Are you two all right?" Ben asked as they approached. "When we saw that canoe . . ."

"We're both okay," Rolfe replied. His hand supported Milly's arm, but her knees felt like jelly and her insides were still in turmoil.

"Are you sure?" Libby demanded. Her face was pale. "What happened?"

"We capsized coming through the rapids," Rolfe said flatly. Milly opened her mouth to correct this version, but his hand tightened on her arm warningly.

"Must have been rough. I'll bet you're both going to be pretty bruised," Ben said.

"Rolfe still has a mark on his face," Libby pointed out.

Milly glanced up in surprise and saw that Libby was right. There was still a livid streak along Rolfe's cheekbone where she had slapped him. Milly felt suddenly lightheaded.

"I don't feel very well," she said abruptly, swallowing hard.

Ben looked at her sympathetically. "Libby's feeling sick to her stomach, too. Must have been something you ate. Why don't you girls get in the canoe and we'll see if we can salvage anything. Then we'll get going. We're going to be late as it is, riding four in one boat."

It was very late that night when Milly finally crept up the stairs to her apartment. The slow trip back to the pickup point, then the hassle of paying for the damaged canoe, coupled with Libby's increasing nausea, had made the ride home anything but pleasant.

"Get some sleep," Rolfe advised as he saw her to the bottom of the stairs. "You've got a big day tomorrow."

"I'll try," Milly murmured. She watched his face uncertainly in the darkness.

"Milly . . ." Rolfe's voice held a husky element. Just then Ben beeped his horn.

"You'd better go," she said.

"Yeah. Tomorrow, then." He hurried back to the waiting car.

Milly spent a restless night filled with frightening dreams that she knew reflected her unresolved feelings for Rolfe. She rose and dressed, concealing the dark circles under her eyes with cover-up, then packed her suitcases. She hadn't forgotten her promise to Gareth to attend the stockholders' meeting the next day, and she would have to make the drive to Little Rock after the auction in order to be on time. It was time for her to be moving on anyway. After today there wouldn't be any reason for her to stay in Altus. The reality of that thought was singularly depressing, for she had grown to love the little town and its people, and Louella, Florie, and Amalie had become the closest thing to a family she had ever had.

But the most upsetting part was Rolfe Hart himself. Milly knew that she should run away as hard and as fast as she could. The memory of his lovemaking was vivid and brought a hot flush to her cheeks. What would have happened if Ben and Libby hadn't come along when they had yesterday? She knew she would have given herself to Rolfe completely, body and soul.

To Milly a sexual relationship was only possible when the emotions were also involved, and a commitment made. Rolfe had hardly uttered a tender word to her, or given any hint of his true feelings, other than an occasional glimpse of his exasperation when she ruffled his cool facade. It did not bode well for the state of Milly's heart. Maybe her precipitate escape to Little Rock was a blessing in disguise. But first she had to pull herself out of this blue funk and do the job she had been hired to do. Straightening her shoulders, Milly set out to do just that.

Milly spent the rest of the morning and early afternoon seeing to a hundred and one details. Early arrivals were already wandering among the rows of neatly laid out items in Rolfe's huge shed. The day was hot and dry, and each car that drove up the narrow road raised another cloud of dust. The women of the Altus Historical Society were doing a brisk business at their refreshment booth as the after-church crowd swelled the ranks of potential customers. It looked as though all of Altus had turned out for the event, as well as quite a few out-of-town visitors.

Milly and the other volunteers from the historical society set up the cashiers' tables and checked the sound system. Amalie and the Abington sisters fluttered here and there, but Milly caught only a brief glimpse of Rolfe and a few of his friends, enlisted by his mother to help load the heavier articles and generally keep order. Then it was nearly time to start the auction.

Milly climbed up the steps of the podium, checked to see that she had her gavel, then turned on the sound system. She felt a trickle of sweat bead along her spine as she reviewed her lists one last time. Even though several large fans circulated the air in the huge barn, it was quite warm. Her sleeveless tailored dress looked cool, but Milly would gladly have rid herself of her hose and heels in exchange for her shorts and T-shirt. She struggled to control a case of the butterflies, knowing that it was just preauction jitters that would vanish as soon as the action began.

"Rubber baby buggy bumpers, rubber baby buggy bumpers," she muttered.

"Lose a baby buggy?" Rolfe paused next to the podium, a puzzled expression on his face.

Milly glanced up and flushed slightly. "Oh, no!" She gave a brittle laugh. She was unsettled by his sudden appearance. "I was warming up. Tongue twisters, you know." She watched Rolfe warily. Why did he have to look so virile and masculine, with his blond hair falling across his broad forehead and his muscular arms straining against the white cotton of his shirt. It ought to be against the law for any man to be so irresistible, she thought peevishly, struggling to slow her hammering pulse. How could she be expected to function when all she wanted to do was press wantonly against his lean body?

"Tongue twisters? I see," Rolfe said, although from

118

his quizzical expression she was sure he didn't. He jammed his fists into his pockets, stretching his jeans tautly across his hips. Milly suppressed a groan. "It's almost time to start," he said. "Are you ready?"

"I hope so," Milly muttered under her breath. She forced a confident smile. "Ready!"

Milly called the crowd to order, gave a brief welcome on behalf of the Altus Historical Society, then began her spiel. She got things rolling by auctioning off a series of smaller items in rapid succession, her lilting, singsong chant keeping rhythmic pace with the excited bidding. It didn't take long for the crowd to get into the swing of things. The tempo picked up over a heated battle for the ownership of an antique button collection, and Milly felt her confidence soar as the crowd interacted with her and enthusiasm abounded. As the larger items came up, things slowed down a bit, but Milly was pleased with the response, at least until Dean Singleton decided to join the fun.

Dean sat conspicuously in the front row, wearing a sports coat the most revolting shade of fuchsia Milly had ever seen. At first his comments seemed directed at the people sitting on either side of him, but as he began to get a few laughs, his voice rose higher and higher.

"A hundred dollars? For that?" he scoffed loudly as a woman nearby bid on an old oak console. "That piece of junk isn't worth ten bucks, Martha!" The woman called Martha faltered, and Milly groaned inwardly. There wasn't anything like a heckler to stop an auction dead in its tracks. And she had the sneaking suspicion that Dean's motive was strictly to spite her for her part in Sebastian's rescue and her friendship with the Abington sisters.

Milly managed to wind up the bidding on the console, but the final amount was much less than she had anticipated. She gritted her teeth and plunged on, but Dean's heckling degenerated into disparaging noises that caused her to bobble her chant embarrassingly on the next item. The bidding declined at an alarming rate.

"Sold!" Milly banged the gavel, then stepped back from the podium ostensibly to get a drink of water for her parched throat. Rolfe joined her at the small table behind the podium and poured her a glass of water from a tall, frosty pitcher.

"Trouble?" Rolfe asked in a low tone.

"Not at all," Milly snapped sarcastically. She knew she was taking out her frustration on Rolfe but was unable to stop herself. "I love it when some dummy disrupts my auction! What burns me up is that he's keeping the bidding low—and it's all for a worthy cause, too!" She tipped the glass up and drank thirstily.

"I'll take care of it," Rolfe said, fixing Singleton with a cold, piercing gaze.

"Oh, no, you don't!" Milly hissed, catching his forearm. She'd be damned if she'd let anyone else fight her battles!

"I'll see that he leaves immediately," Rolfe said grimly.

The pressure of Milly's hand was a tantalizing reminder of his loss of control the previous day. God, how he wanted this woman! Milly had to be the most infuriating, intriguing woman he had ever met, and together they were as explosive as nitroglycerin! It was a situation doubly disturbing because Rolfe had always prided himself on his level-headedness and iron control. His disastrous affair with Monique had taught him well the value of self-control, yet even now he could almost feel the light weight of Milly's supple form as it pressed against him, the brush of her breasts

120

as they flattened against his chest. And that mouth, so sweet and generous . . .

Rolfe reluctantly moved his attention from Milly's lips to the words she was forming.

"This is my problem, Rolfe," she insisted. "I'll take care of Mr. Singleton in my own way."

"Spare me your methods." Rolfe shuddered. "We don't need another disaster. What do you plan to do, slap a pair of handcuffs on him? Or gig him with a fishhook?"

"Oh, you—" Milly bit her lip as angry words threatened to spill out. She controlled herself with an effort, but she was fuming inwardly. "You just mind your own business! I don't need your help!" She drew an angry breath and stared him up and down with outraged eyes. "Don't you ever change your shirt?" she flung at him.

"What . . . ?" Rolfe's expression reflected his befuddlement as he gazed down at his shirt. What did this crazy woman have against white shirts, anyway? But before Rolfe could react to this unexpected attack, Milly returned to the podium and determinedly began her description of the next item.

Rolfe stepped back and folded his arms across his chest. All right, he thought grimly, let her do her worst! Milly began her chant, expertly picking up on the slight movements, the raised eyebrow, the tug of an earlobe that signified another bid.

"What horror movie you suppose that came from?" Dean Singleton's voice carried over the rapidly articulated chanting.

"Is that an increase of fifty, Mr. Singleton?" Milly asked without breaking her stride.

Dean looked up, startled, but his sharp negative movement only increased his bid again.

"Upping your own bid, Mr. Singleton? How very

generous of you! The historical society appreciates it very much! Going once, twice, sold! To Mr. Singleton for one hundred fifty dollars! I'm sure you'll enjoy this very attractive elephant's foot ottoman. Now, our next item . . ."

Reluctantly Rolfe's lips twitched once, then he held his expression still by sheer willpower. Singleton's protests were drowned by Milly's throaty chant. That was, until she accepted his loudly voiced opposition to his new acquisition as a bid of three hundred dollars for the motheaten moose head now on the block!

After that every time Dean Singleton opened his mouth, or rubbed an agitated hand through his thinning hair, or made a gesture of disgust, he found himself the proud new owner of a growing collection of particularly unattractive items.

From his vantage point behind the podium, Rolfe watched the grinning audience enjoy the spectacle. Ben, camera in hand, stood on the fringes of the crowd next to Libby, and he took several pictures for the newspaper, including a close-up of Dean's blustering countenance. Every time Rolfe caught his friend's eye, it was all he could do not to laugh out loud.

Finally Dean was forced to beat a strategic retreat, but not before he had also acquired an atrocious Victorian horn hat rack, a ratty bearskin rug, and a Flemish tapestry that must have weighed no less than four hundred pounds and took three men to carry to his car.

"Leaving so soon, Mr. Singleton?" Milly asked from the podium as Dean paid his tab at the cashiers' table. Her lips curved into a gleeful smile. "The historical society is grateful for your donation! How about that, everyone? Let's give Mr. Singleton a hand for being such a good sport."

The crowd applauded politely as Dean retired from

the field in ignominious defeat, his wallet empty and his face a bright red that clashed with his jacket. After that there were no further misadventures, and the bidding continued smoothly until Milly wearily banged her gavel on the final item. She was almost nostalgic as the enormous old armoire fell under her hammer. Rolfe had taken her into his arms of his own free will beside that armoire. But she swallowed her sentiments and resolutely announced it "going, going, gone!"

The crowd broke up, some heading to the cashiers' desk to claim their merchandise, others out the doors to the parking lot. Milly climbed down from the podium as people crowded around her to offer their congratulations.

"You were great, Milly!" Ben crowed. He pounded her on the back as Libby beamed.

"Thanks, Ben," Milly said. "You got a good deal on the pressed-back rocking chair."

"It is pretty, isn't it?" Libby responded. "And I didn't have to twist Ben's arm too hard, either. He was too busy laughing!"

"I'm afraid I got carried away," Milly said worriedly. "But Mr. Singleton made me so angry! And I don't like the way he tries to intimidate the Abington sisters. I wanted to teach him a lesson."

"His empty wallet proves he's a slow learner," Ben said with a chuckle. "Did you see his face when he realized he'd bought that moose head?" This sent Ben off into fresh gales of laughter.

"No doubt Dean is plotting revenge this very moment," Rolfe added, joining the group.

Milly stiffened, her ire at Rolfe rising anew. "Since I won't be around to find out what it is, I'm not worried," she snapped.

"Oh, Milly, you don't mean you're planning to leave already?" Libby cried.

Milly shrugged and shot Rolfe a cool look. "There's nothing to keep me here now. Excuse me, I want to speak to Amalie."

She moved away, her heart twisting in her breast. She felt as though she were about to explode with pent-up emotions. It appeared Rolfe wouldn't give any sign that he wanted her to stay. The pain of his apparent rejection made her reckless.

"She can't mean that," Libby protested. "Rolfe, do something!"

Rolfe's expression was distant. "What do you want me to do, Lib?" he asked quietly. "She's a grown woman. I guess it's about time I realized that."

Then he walked away, too, leaving Ben and Libby gaping after both of them in dismay.

"Oh, there you are, dear," Amalie cried, rushing over to envelop Milly in a warm hug. "You were marvelous, simply marvelous! The treasurer just told me the historical society cleared over seven thousand dollars today!"

"I'm so glad," Milly murmured.

"Florie and Louella want to congratulate you, too," Amalie said, leading her over to where the Abington sisters sat.

"Milly, you were splendid," Louella said. "Especially the way you handled that annoying man!"

"Thank you."

"Yes, indeed," Florie agreed, smiling benignly. The elderly women exchanged a significant look.

"In fact," Louella continued, her wrinkled face settling into satisfied lines, "Florie and I have decided you are the answer to our prayers!"

Milly would have sworn she had more sense than to be bamboozled, sweet-talked, and browbeaten by two little old ladies. But two nights later, as she steered the jeep once again down the familiar streets of Altus, she realized she had never had a chance. She should have seized the opportunity and run like hell away from Altus, Rolfe Hart, and two women full of arsenic and old lace. They hadn't even played fair! She'd had her chance to make a clean getaway, but now here she was heading straight back into the lion's den!

"It's a matter of being practical," Louella had explained. "Despite the things we donated to the auction, the house is fairly bursting at the seams with things we have no further need of. That is why we would like to hire you!"

"But, Louella, I don't see—" Milly began as a sense of impending disaster closed in on her.

"It's simple," Louella explained briskly. "We need someone knowledgeable to inventory the contents of our home, then supervise the sale of selected items. I daresay whatever return we receive will help placate Mr. Jenkins at the bank or be of use in the upkeep of the vineyards. Heaven knows there's always something that needs doing!"

Milly remembered from her original tour of the house that the unused rooms were indeed crammed full of almost every conceivable item that a family of many generations might cast off. And underneath the dust and cobwebs, Milly had seen things that piqued her interest. There might be a few real treasures among the mountains of trash.

But it wasn't just her interest that decided Milly, in the long run. It was the fact that the Abington sisters obviously needed her help desperately. Wrapped in their secure cocoon of aging gentility, they were sure to be taken to the cleaners should they try to sell any of their treasures on their own. And despite their polite fiction, it was clear that the money was a major consideration. She'd just have to put her personal feelings aside for a while. She had racked her brain for a way to help Louella and Florie, and now that a solution had fallen into her lap, she couldn't turn her back on them.

Gareth had thought her crazy to be heading back to Altus, too. She had sat beside him during the stockholders' meeting, trying to look as though she was a responsible board member. There had been a crush of reporters to avoid, as usual, but in her severely tailored suit, she hoped she had appeased Jonathan's sense of formality.

"Just wish you'd find a perch and light somewhere," Jonathan had grumbled as he received her obligatory peck on the cheek. "It's damned inconvenient having to track you down!"

"You know you don't need me." Milly had laughed easily, but the words produced a pang in her heart. What would it be like to really be needed by someone? The idea was attractive, but frightening. She sighed. It was highly unlikely that competent, assured Rolfe would ever need her, except in the physical sense, and for Milly that wasn't enough.

She supposed that running away was a cowardly solution, anyway. It seemed fate meant her to face the problem of her relationship with Rolfe head on. She'd simply have to make it clear that despite their mutual attraction, there was nothing substantial between them. With that thought firmly in mind, she pulled into the Abington driveway. It was late, but a single light burned in the house. She grabbed her purse and a parcel and headed for the stairs to her apartment.

"Milly, wait!"

Rolfe's voice made Milly hesitate halfway up the staircase. He crossed the garden from the back porch of the house, where he had been waiting. With a feeling of rising panic, Milly continued to the top of the stairs and inserted her key in the door. So much for good intentions, she thought in disgust.

Rolfe bounded up the stairs after her two at a time. "Didn't you hear me?" he asked, irritated.

Milly flicked on the light switches, flooding the interior and the tiny landing with light. She set her things down, then hurried back out on the landing.

"Hello, Rolfe," she said. The yellow bands of light cast wayward shadows across Rolfe's serious expression, but Milly dodged past him before he could say anything further. Her heels clattered down the stairs, and she cursed the narrow suit skirt that inhibited her movements. Rolfe frowned as she brushed past, then followed her back down the stairs.

"I want to talk to you," he said.

Milly juggled her two suitcases, and stuck the edge of a paper bag between her teeth. "So talk," she said, her voice muffled. She headed back up the stairs. Rolfe had no option but to follow her.

"For God's sake, will you be still just one minute?" he asked in exasperation. "Here, let me take that." Milly paused midway up the stairs and let him have the largest suitcase, then removed the bag from between her teeth.

"Thanks." They reached the door of the apartment once again. Milly reached for her suitcase. "I'm tired, Rolfe. What is it you want?"

"What do I want? I've been waiting for you for hours! I want to know what the hell you think you're doing!"

"I don't know what you're talking about," Milly said wearily. Her shoulders slumped beneath the silk of her bow blouse. It was clear he wasn't very happy to see her again. She felt close to tears.

"You don't have a grain of sense! You know that the

127

Abington sisters haven't got an extra nickel, don't you?"

"Oh, that," she said tonelessly. "I know it."

"Then what are you trying to do?"

"I'm trying to help them!" Milly snapped, losing her temper. Anger was a better defense against the desolation tearing her heart apart.

"You know they can't afford to pay you anything. How do you propose to live?" He ran an agitated hand through his hair. He had been worried sick over Milly's sudden disappearance, and then aghast to find out from Amalie that Milly had agreed to another lame-brained scheme!

"I'm working on commission," Milly said coolly. "Not that it's any of your business. There are a lot of things you don't know about me, Rolfe. I've managed to live well enough for twenty-six years. I think I can manage it a little longer without you trying to play big brother."

"Big brother!" Rolfe shook his head. "You're as green as grass, despite your advanced years," he said sarcastically. "Who do you think you are, the Lone Ranger? Stray dogs, jewel thieves, and now little old ladies! Woman, you need a keeper!"

"And I suppose you're applying for the position?" Milly asked angrily. "Well, thanks, but no thanks!" She took a step back and slammed the door in Rolfe's startled face. Rolfe raised a fist to pound on the door, but it swung open again and a brightly colored garment sailed out, hitting him squarely in the face.

"Take that, you stuffed shirt!" Milly shouted. "And I hope you choke on it!" The door slammed once more resoundingly.

Rolfe removed the fabric enveloping his face, then stared in shocked horror at the garment. It was a shirt, but what a shirt! Bird-of-paradise flowers in riotous colors of turquoise and green slashed across the brilliant crimson of its background. Rolfe was afraid to look at it too long for fear of permanent blindness, yet he couldn't seem to tear his horrified gaze away from it. Suddenly his anger deflated like a popped balloon. His mouth softened into a grudging smile. Leave it to Milly to illustrate a message with flair! He knocked on the closed door.

"Milly, open this door!"

"Go 'way."

The muffled voice sounded strange to his ears. Rolfe leaned a broad shoulder against the door and tapped lightly. "Milly? Are you all right? Let me in."

"No!"

"Milly! Open this door, or I swear I'll break it down," he promised. Silence. "All right! You asked for it!" he warned her with a grin. He stepped away from the door. "Here I come! One, two . . ." He heard a frightened squeak, then the knob turned and the door opened a crack. He caught the edge of the door and pushed against her slight resistance. His voice was gentle. "Please, Milly, let me come in."

Milly released the door and stepped back, hastily wiping her cheeks. Rolfe frowned, the outlandish tropical shirt casually draped across one shoulder.

"Hey, you're crying," he said in amazement.

"I'm not!" she denied. She glared at him, but her full lower lip trembled. "I'm just mad!"

Rolfe used the hem of the brilliant shirt to dry her eyes, his touch tender. "I didn't mean to make you cry."

Milly drew in a shaky breath. "I know." She shivered when Rolfe leaned down and pressed a chaste kiss on her forehead.

"I'm sorry," he murmured.

Milly quivered at his touch, and her eyes closed.

129

"It's all right," she whispered. She heard the swish of clothing and opened her eyes in alarm. "What are you doing?"

"I want to try on my present." Rolfe swiftly unbuttoned his ever-present white shirt. He tossed it carelessly aside, then shrugged into the scarlet replacement. "Well, what do you think?"

"It—it will take some getting used to," Milly admitted finally. Rolfe looked exotic but totally masculine in the bright shirt.

"Do you think you could?" Rolfe asked softly, taking her into his arms. Milly's lips parted and moved soundlessly as she tried to express the unnamed emotion filling her chest and constricting her heart. "I'll take that for a yes," Rolfe murmured.

His head lowered and his lips covered hers. From that moment she was lost—lost to the tenderness of his kiss, the burning flame of his mounting passion. It was not enough to press against him. She wanted to be part of him.

Her mouth opened to the seeking pressure of his tongue, and her arms curled around his neck as he pulled her into the cradle of his thighs. Her breasts pressed against his muscular chest, the thin silk of her blouse no barrier between their beating hearts.

It was a beautiful dream, and Milly never wanted to waken.

CHAPTER EIGHT

"Promise me you'll never disappear like that again," Rolfe whispered against her ear. "I nearly went crazy." His breath was warm on Milly's skin and his hands stroked her back, then tangled in the silky mass of her dark hair.

"I didn't know," Milly murmured. Her cheek was pressed against his broad chest, and his unique male scent rose to her nostrils, sending coherent thought flying from her brain. Rolfe's large hands gently tugged her hair, tipping her face up to his. Milly saw his surprised frown.

"Didn't know?"

"Whether or not you cared if you ever saw me again," she whispered. Her hands held him around the waist underneath the loose hem of the tropical shirt.

"How could you think that?" he wondered.

"You never said—" Milly broke off, unsure how to go on. Her need for him was an aching hunger.

Rolfe took a deep breath. "I know, honey. Sometimes it's hard for me to express how I feel," he admitted, his voice ragged and regretful. "But I thought I'd *shown* you in a hundred different ways."

"Maybe you'd better show me once more," Milly said softly.

"With pleasure." His smile was tender. Slowly he untied the bow of her blouse, then worked his way down the row of buttons. Milly watched his eyes in breathless wonder as their azure blue began to darken with his growing desire. His fingertips were slightly rough against her skin, catching on the filmy fabric of her shirt as he slipped it from her creamy shoulders. His mouth followed his hands, sending tremors of desire through Milly as he lightly brushed her slip straps down her arms, then teased her naked breasts with the softest of caresses.

Milly swayed against him and pressed a kiss against the broad wall of his chest in return. The curling chest hairs tickled her lips, and she felt Rolfe's swift gasp of pleasure when her tongue found the flat coin of his nipple.

He groaned, then his hands were suddenly clumsy, fumbling at the clasp and zipper of her skirt until it dropped away with the slip. His mouth descended, capturing hers in a hungry, ravishing kiss that she answered with heat of her own. Rolfe's arms wrapped around her, lifting her free of her skirt, and he carried her toward the bedroom without releasing her lips.

He threw back the covers on the bed, then laid Milly gently on the sheets. He drew back, his eyes molten as he took in her unselfconscious beauty and the unabashed need he saw mirrored in her hooded green eyes. Silently he sat at her feet, lifting one small foot and placing it flat against his chest. Milly's breath sighed from her lungs as he slowly pulled her pantyhose down the length of first one leg, then the other. She felt her flesh melting under the heated warmth of his hands as she lay naked and waiting for him.

"It's not fair," she whispered.

"What?"

"You have too many clothes on. I want to touch

132

you," she said, not afraid to show her impatience for him. She heard Rolfe's deep chuckle of delight.

"That can easily be remedied," he said, sliding out of his new shirt and stripping off his slacks and briefs with an economy of motion. Then he lay beside her and gathered her tenderly into his strong embrace.

Milly traced the perfection of his lean body with her trembling hands. His shoulders were broad, his hips lean and muscled, his stomach flat and lightly downed with darker hair that thickened at the top of his thighs and around the rampant proof of his manhood.

"I've needed this," Rolfe said. "It feels so right to have you in my arms." His fingers circled the tip of her breast, teasing the rosy nipple into turgid blossom.

"Yes," Milly breathed. Rolfe's hand caressed the delicate length of her collarbone, then the elegant line of her neck. His fingers paused at her nape, and Milly felt his smile.

"Will you humor me?" he asked.

Milly looked at him questioningly, then gave him a languid smile. This was a Rolfe she did not know, and the temptation to discover him was too great to resist. Sensing her willingness, Rolfe pulled away, shifting her so that she lay on her stomach. With exquisite sensuality he pushed her hair away from her nape, then kissed the sensitive skin on the back of her neck. His tongue explored the texture of her skin until Milly shivered uncontrollably. "I've been wanting to do that since the day we met," Rolfe said, his voice thick.

"It feels—feels—" Milly was burning up and freezing cold at the same time.

"Do you want me to stop?"

"No-o," Milly panted. Her face was hidden in her folded arms and her voice was muffled. She quivered as Rolfe chuckled, then let his lips travel the length of her spine, settle briefly on the softness of her buttocks, then rest tantalizingly at the back of her knee. She was mindless with the sensations his questing lips evoked and made no demur when he encouraged her to roll over. Then he began his excruciating journey back up her body, teasing the quivering flesh of her inner thighs, then exploring the hollow of her navel, and finally feasting on the lushness of her swollen breasts. She clutched convulsively at his shoulders, dragging him closer.

"Rolfe, what are you doing to me?" she asked hoarsely, her head falling back. Rolfe smoothed the jut of her hipbone, then tested the soft, moist petals of her womanhood with his fingertips. Milly arched against his hand. He groaned at the liquid heat of her that proclaimed her readiness for him.

"Trying to make you want me as much as I want you," he said against her breast.

"I do. Oh, Rolfe, please kiss me!" she begged. Her lips met his in a fevered kiss. His knee parted her thighs, then he was part of her, and Milly thought she would surely burst with the sweet pleasure of him.

Rolfe moved against her, full of strength and power tempered by his awareness of her. Milly opened herself completely to him, trying to take him ever deeper to return the pleasure he gave her. Mutual consideration changed their lovemaking from a mere physical union to a sublime communion where for a time they were truly one entity.

Milly arched against Rolfe and called his name as the heavens exploded above her. She felt his final triumphant thrust against her, and exulted in their rapture, clutching his back as the earth righted itself and their breathing gradually slowed.

Rolfe moved from her reluctantly, showering her face with kisses and love nips and nuzzling her earlobe. Milly murmured sleepily and curled up next to him.

"I take it all back," Milly said, her lashes fanning down across her cheekbones. Rolfe gazed adoringly at the dewy lips, the flushed curve of her cheeks framed by sweat-dampened tendrils of dark hair.

"All what, love?" he asked lazily.

"Every mean, rotten thing I ever thought about you. Especially the part about your being a big brother. There's nothing brotherly about what you do to me," she murmured. "Nothing at all."

Her breathing became regular, and Rolfe knew she was asleep in his arms. It suddenly occurred to him that it was where she had always belonged.

Milly woke slowly and stretched luxuriously. She was filled with a delicious sense of well-being that owed everything to Rolfe Hart. What a continual surprise he was! Before he had left at dawn, he had come to her twice more, astonishing her with the rising levels of sensuality and the sensitive nature of his love-play.

He had laughed tenderly at her exhaustion as he kissed her good-bye. By contrast, he seemed full of energy and ready to meet the new day. His hand had cupped the curve of her hip possessively, and he reluctantly drew back despite her welcoming smile. He had work at the winery that wouldn't wait, but he promised to see her in the evening.

Milly sat up, her hair a dark, tousled cloud. She grinned down at the garment she wore—Rolfe's white shirt. She wasn't quite sure how she had come to be wearing it, but she chuckled softly as she realized Rolfe must be wearing the tropical shirt. That ought to make everyone sit up and take notice!

Happiness bubbled up inside Milly, and she hugged

herself to contain her effervescent elation. Euphoria filled her. She was in love with Rolfe! And, after last night, she knew he cared for her, too. No man could ever have been as attentive, or as tender, otherwise. Milly could hardly restrain her impatience to be near him again. She climbed out of bed, eager to begin her day.

A short time later Milly had bathed and dressed in a brief strapless playsuit, piling her hair in a loose Gibson girl knot on top of her head for coolness. She drank a quick cup of instant coffee, then hurried over to the Abington house, amazed that it was already mid-morning. She had a lot to do, and sitting around dreaming about Rolfe was no way to get it done, no matter how pleasant the prospect.

"Are you certain you won't have a cup of coffee?" Florie asked a few minutes later in the kitchen. "I know you must be tired after getting in so late last night."

"No, I'm fine," Milly assured her.

"Rolfe waited for a time last night," Louella said, setting her coffee cup in the old-fashioned enamel sink. "He must have gone home before you arrived."

"Be careful, Lulu," Florie said, fussing about the sink. "You know how coffee stains this old thing. What I wouldn't give for a modern kitchen! Buford put new Formica in his cottage last month. Looks so nice, too."

"Hush, Florie. I want to ask Milly if she talked to Rolfe," Louella chided. She turned again to Milly as Florie muttered and ran hot water over the dishes. "I saw Rolfe's truck early this morning. Did you see him, Milly? He was most concerned. In fact, he would have been on his way to Little Rock after you if we hadn't mentioned that you were coming right back."

"Ah, yes, I saw him," Milly stammered. She felt a

bit flustered with the pleasurable knowledge that Rolfe would have followed her after all. This, and the fact that Louella hadn't realized that Rolfe had spent the night, made her cheeks burn, but the sisters didn't seem to notice.

"Funny thing, though," Louella added vaguely. "He was wearing some sort of red shirt. I don't recall that I've ever seen Rolfe dressed in anything flashy."

"Surely you're mistaken, Lulu dear," Florie said.

Milly almost choked on her suppressed laughter. "I'll get started on the inventory," she said hastily, her voice strangled. "Any particular place you'd like me to start?"

"Anywhere is fine, dear," Louella replied, waving her off into the upper regions of the house.

Nearly two hours later Milly had compiled quite a list of items. The wealth of Victorian furniture and incidental pieces stored in the closed bedrooms was substantial. With careful marketing, their sale would fetch a hefty sum. And she hadn't even begun to explore the gabled attics.

"It won't be any problem to sell these things," Milly told Louella enthusiastically when she came downstairs. "For instance, that carved mahogany whatnot stand could bring over a thousand dollars."

"That was always Grandmother Patton's favorite piece," Florie said with a mournful sigh. "She bought it as a bride."

"I don't think we could part with it," Louella said with a frown. "For sentimental reasons, you understand." Milly was a bit taken aback, but the women watched her expectantly from their seats in the charming but shabby living room. The low drone of their favorite soap opera sounded from the small television in the corner.

"Well, that's understandable, of course," Milly said.

"But there are many other things. There's a large bedstead with red velvet padding—"

"Uncle Horatio paid twenty-five dollars for that," Florie reminisced. "It must have been about 1917."

"No, Florie, dear. Horatio didn't return from the first war until 1918," Louella corrected.

"What about the rosewood bow-front chest of drawers in the third bedroom?" Milly asked, beginning to feel a bit desperate.

"Part of Mama's trousseau," Louella declared. "We couldn't possibly bear to part with *that!*" The phone shrilled in the hall, and Florie hefted her plump bulk out of her chair and went to answer it.

"But Louella," Milly protested. "The whole point is to sell something! You need the money more than the furniture!"

"We couldn't bear to sell some of our things to total strangers. On the other hand, if we knew they would be with someone who could appreciate their history, it might be different. Don't give up yet, dear," Louella said serenely, reaching over to turn up the sound of the television. "I'm sure you'll find something."

"Milly, dear, telephone," Florie called, and Milly escaped, grateful for the interruption.

"Rolfe?" she asked into the receiver and heard a delighted feminine laugh on the other end of the line.

"Sorry to disappoint you. It's just me—Libby! How about coming to lunch to ease your disappointment?" her friend suggested.

"You're on!"

A short time later, sitting in Libby's comfortable country kitchen amid the copper pots and gingham curtains, Milly tried to explain her concern about the Abington sisters.

"I just don't know what to do with them," she said in exasperation.

138

"I'm sure they'll come around if their situation is really as precarious as it seems," Libby said comfortingly. She set a large chef's salad topped with a generous amount of pink Thousand Island dressing in front of Milly. "I'm just glad that they gave you a reason to stay with us a while longer. The Grape Festival is this week and I wanted to ask you a favor . . ." Libby trailed off as Milly dragged a hunk of cheese through the dressing and happily began to munch. Libby blanched and backed away from the table. She sat down hard in the pressed-back rocker she had bought at the auction, which now held a place of honor near a bay-fronted window. "Ohh!"

"Libby, what's wrong?" Milly was on her feet in an instant, alarmed at the whiteness in Libby's face.

Libby waved weakly. "I'm all right. It's just that the sight and smell of food right now . . ." She shook her bright red curls apologetically and pressed her small hands against her middle in a protective gesture.

"You're pregnant!" Milly cried, eyes wide.

Libby nodded, and her smile was madonnalike.

"That's wonderful!" Milly said.

"We think so. But it's a bit inconvenient right now, because I was supposed to be in charge of the food and decorations for the masked ball. It's the first time we've ever had a costume party, and I wanted to do it right."

"Say no more! I'll be glad to do whatever you need," Milly said. She grinned as she reseated herself. "Is it all right if I eat my salad now that you've gotten what you wanted?"

"Milly! I didn't mean, I mean I . . ." Libby sputtered.

"Just kidding." Milly giggled. "I don't mind helping at all."

"You're a good friend." Libby sighed. "I just hope

we can keep you around. If Rolfe would just come to his senses—Did I say something wrong?''

Milly felt her cheeks blazing and stuffed a forkful of lettuce into her mouth to hide her discomfiture. "Rolfe?" she asked, chewing determinedly.

"Don't try to kid me," Libby said with a laugh. "It's quite obvious to everyone that there's something going on between you two."

Milly set down her fork. "To everyone?" she asked in horror.

"To everyone who cares about you and Rolfe," Libby replied softly. "Don't worry, I'm not going to ask you anything else, but be kind to him, won't you, Milly? I'd hate to see either one of you get hurt." Then Libby began to talk of other things, including the Grape Festival and the preparations for the masked ball, but most definitely not about Rolfe and Milly.

Be kind to Rolfe? As Milly worked in the attic that afternoon, she wondered if that was possible. The rosy euphoria that had surrounded her was beginning to wear off, and she was troubled. Maybe the kindest thing she could do for Rolfe was get out of his life altogether. The thought was followed instantly by a shaft of such searing pain that Milly had to sit down on top of a dusty trunk.

Dust motes floated lazily in the yellow shaft of afternoon sunlight angling through the grimy panes of the narrow dormer windows. Trunks and boxes spilled their contents onto the plank floor, evidence of Milly's work. The attic was warm but not unbearably hot, because Milly had opened several of the windows and a dry breeze circulated through the narrow spaces. A dusty pier mirror gleamed with reflected light in one corner, and a wire dress form stood cocked at a drunken angle in another. Dusty sheets covered a

140

worn roll-back velvet chaise near the door leading to a narrow flight of stairs down from the attic.

Milly sighed, then rose and opened the trunk. She had already uncovered a miscellany of old clothing and hats, dishes, and bric-a-brac that could be sold to collectors, but she felt too depressed to hope that Louella and Florie would decide to part with any of them. The sisters would continue to drift along until circumstances jolted them into harsh reality. She knew she could use some of her own resources to help them, perhaps an anonymous donation, but she also knew the sisters were just as likely to refuse a gift like that on sheer principle. So the lovely old house would continue to crumble, and no laughing children would ever play again on its wide porches. If only she and Rolfe. . . . Milly shook her head and thrust the tempting vision away. It was too soon to start building dream castles.

Brittle tissue paper rustled as Milly unloaded the trunk. It was mostly clothing in surprisingly good condition, but it hardly held her attention until she reached the bottom of the trunk. Then she gave a gasp of pleasure and reverently lifted out the most exquisite dress she had ever seen.

It was a wedding gown of Victorian style, its soft muslin aged to a delicate ecru color. A high stand-up collar and mutton-leg sleeves gave it an aura of virginal purity. Bands of fragile lace and intricate tucks adorned the bodice and flowed down the full skirt. Milly held the dress up to the light, and the fragrance of dried lavender filled her nostrils.

Furtively Milly glanced around the empty attic, then gave in to temptation. She slipped out of her strapless playsuit, then put on the gown, being careful of its many buttons and ancient seams. The soft, aged fabric clung like a second skin, outlining the upward thrust of her naked breasts, then falling from her hips in gentle folds. She moved forward to gaze at the figure from the past reflected in the spotted pier mirror. The graceful woman who looked back with wide green eyes was a beautiful stranger.

Milly lightly touched the lace of the tall collar at her slender neck, almost afraid to breathe. Tendrils of dark hair fell around her face, and the casual upswept bun was suddenly elegant. She turned slowly this way and that, admiring the fantasy. A soft gasp caused her to turn, and she found Rolfe watching her from the top of the stairs like an intent acolyte viewing a mystery for the first time.

Milly's lips parted as Rolfe walked slowly toward her, but no words came out. His golden hair gleamed briefly when he passed through a sunbeam, and his eyes were so blue Milly felt a strange desire to weep. A deep magenta knit shirt accentuated the muscular breadth of his shoulders, and his long legs were encased in crisply creased tan slacks. She lifted her chin slightly so that she could see his face when he stopped in front of her. His knuckles grazed the curve of her cheekbone in a gentle caress. His gaze melded with hers for a timeless moment. Then his mouth brushed hers, warm and dry, and utterly exciting.

"Oh, God, you're beautiful."

Milly's heart slammed against her chest at Rolfe's softly spoken words, then raced unmercifully. His lips caught hers in a fiery kiss, and his fingertips trailed restlessly down the front of the gown. Milly's nipples contracted, thrusting through the thin lawn of the bodice. He laughed softly, triumphant at her involuntary response. His deft fingers found the covered buttons at the back of the dress and swiftly began to unfasten them. Milly's heart hammered in her throat, and her breathing became uneven.

Rolfe slid the gown from her shoulders so that it dropped at her feet. He caught her close and his kiss deepened, his tongue probing and questing as her breasts flattened against his chest. His hands roamed arousingly down her back and slipped into her panties. Milly quivered in his arms, need and the heat of his mouth overriding everything else. He slid his arm under her knees and picked her up.

"What are you doing?" she gasped weakly. Rolfe strode over to the chaise and pulled the dusty sheet free with one hand. He laid Milly down on the threadbare green velvet upholstery and grinned wickedly.

"What do you think?"

Milly came suddenly upright, a look of sheer amazement on her face. "You can't! We can't!" She laughed, incredulous. "The old ladies would have a coronary!" Rolfe stripped off his shirt and quietly pulled shut the attic door and shot the bolt home.

"What they don't know . . ."

"Rolfe!" Milly was totally aghast.

"Now who's being too conventional?" he growled, lowering himself beside her and forcing her back.

"You're shameless," Milly accused, then moaned as his lips gently sucked the rosy bud of one breast.

"Where you're concerned, always," Rolfe rasped. His nimble fingers pulled the last impediment to his desire free of her hips, then he shed his remaining clothes in unaccustomed haste.

Milly's pulse accelerated when he touched her again, smoothing her curves in a slow, sensual caress that left her reeling. He whispered soft love words into the shell of her ear, then his lips traveled down her neck, sending tingles of delight flaring to her extremities. Milly stroked the contours of his back, illuminated in strips by the dusty slanting rays of the afternoon sun. Her nails raked his flesh reflexively when his tongue again found a sensitive nipple. He circled the turgid nub, laving the swollen flesh, then drew it into the hot, moist cavern of his mouth and sucked gently.

"Rolfe," she murmured, every pore crying out for more of him. Her hands slid down his hips, reached for him, touched him intimately. She felt his swift gasp of pleasure, then they were both eager, moved together, became one.

The late afternoon heat was nothing to compare to their desire as they soared upward on a mindless spiral of passion. The rough hairiness of Rolfe's chest rasped against Milly's sensitized skin, a contrast to the soft old velvet under her back. Their legs twined and they were locked in a dizzying, thrusting embrace that left no room for mere thought. Suddenly their wild ride flung them into an oblivion of pleasure, a throbbing fulfillment that scattered their senses and left them spent and drenched with sweat.

There was no sound then but the soft rasping of ragged breaths. Rolfe's cheek rested between Milly's breasts as he tried to restore his breathing to a regular rhythm. Milly was too groggy with physical satisfaction to do more than thread her fingers through his thick golden hair. Reluctantly, after a long while, they moved apart. They dressed, laughing softly as they located their scattered clothing. Milly's hair had tumbled down about her shoulders, and she looked young and oddly defenseless as she sat on the chaise. Rolfe cupped the side of her face and kissed her tenderly.

"I'll never get enough of you," he murmured. Milly smiled, her eyes luminous. Rolfe's expression was suddenly serious. He hesitated, then plunged ahead. "Milly, will you marry me?"

"What?" Milly's single word was a soft gasp, and her expression was stunned.

Rolfe's arms curled around her and he pulled her close. "I love you, Milly. Say yes."

"Oh, Rolfe!" she whispered, her eyes shining, her face radiant with joy. "I—I never expected this."

"What, marriage?" he asked, a wry smile quirking his sensual mouth. "Isn't that where a serious relationship should lead, especially for a man as 'conventional' as I am? After what's happened between us, what else could you think?"

"I didn't think."

"That's typical." Rolfe's smile was indulgent. "Well, what do you say?"

"Yes!" Milly exclaimed, flinging her arms around his neck and showering his face with kisses in an ecstasy of happiness. "Oh, Rolfe, yes!"

"Oh, Milly," he said, then swallowed hard on the welling of emotion that threatened to clog his throat. His smile was a trifle crooked. "When do you want to get married?"

"How about this afternoon?" Milly returned. Her loving smile widened at Rolfe's chuckle. "Tomorrow?" She leaned over and nuzzled the base of his neck.

"Your eagerness is very flattering, my love," he said, his voice humorous. "But I'm afraid the arrangements will take a couple of days at least. Do you want the wedding here or in Little Rock?"

"Here." Milly's voice was muffled as she kissed Rolfe's earlobe, delicately nipping at it with her teeth.

Rolfe caught her shoulders, his chest heaving with suppressed laughter. "Woman, be serious for one minute! Isn't there anyone you'd want to invite?"

"I think kissing the man I love is deadly serious," Milly replied mischievously. Her fingertip glided over the outline of Rolfe's mouth. He kissed her finger. Milly's voice softened, became husky. "I do love you, you know."

"Yes, I suppose I do, but it's nice to hear." Rolfe gave her a squeeze. "Now, as for the guest list . . ."

"Back to business, eh? Well," she mused, "I suppose I should notify Jonathan, and Gareth, of course. Lord, the lawyers will have a field day with this!"

"Who's Jonathan, and what about lawyers?" Rolfe's tone was faintly amused.

Milly slipped her arms around his waist and pressed her cheek against his chest. "Oh, Rolfe, I'm so glad you're who you are!"

"What are you talking about?" Rolfe's indulgent chuckle was mixed with exasperation.

"Because it won't matter to you."

"*What* won't matter? And what lawyers?" he asked, tipping her face up so he could see her expression.

"It's sort of complicated to explain," she began hesitantly. "I have some business obligations because of property I inherited from my parents. But it doesn't matter really, because all I want is to marry you, and raise grapes and children . . ."

"How much property?"

"Kind of a lot," she admitted. She shot him a sideways glance, biting her lip on a half-smile. "What would you say if you found out you'd just made love to the richest woman in four states?"

Rolfe began to laugh. "Milly! You and your jokes! You really had me going there for a minute!" His laughter died off at her rueful expression. "You're not kidding, are you?"

Milly shook her head. "I'm afraid not. But that's why I'm so happy! You're such a wonderful man, and not a bit neurotic, so my having a little money of my own won't possibly present any problems!"

"What does 'a little money' mean? I wondered

when Mother mentioned a Swiss finishing school."
Rolfe drew away a little, his voice edged with caution.

"Oh, that was Uncle Howard's idea," Milly said dismissively. "I think it was his way of making sure I didn't disgrace him at the debutante balls."

"You were a debutante, too?"

"Well, sure, but it was such a drag. The boys who were our escorts were all from those old inbred families. You know the type—stoop-shouldered, pimply-faced brains or else zero-IQ jocks."

"So your family is wealthy? Old money, I take it?"

"Well, there's wealthy and then there's *wealthy,*" Milly replied nervously. She took a deep breath. "Rolfe, I own Carter Petroleum."

The attic was silent, and Milly watched Rolfe with growing apprehension. He straightened, and his hands dropped away from her shoulders. There was suddenly more than physical distance between them.

"I'd call that wealthy," Rolfe said slowly. His tone was flat.

"Well, it's not like I had a choice about it," Milly said defensively. She was frightened of the sudden chilliness in Rolfe's blue gaze.

"So you didn't think something like that was important enough to tell me?" he asked.

"Well, I suppose it's important, but—"

"And you'd let us go on indefinitely under false pretenses?"

"False pretenses? No, that's not true at all!" she denied heatedly, but a sharp finger of guilt pinched her conscience. Hadn't she feared all along that something like this would happen? But how could she make him understand that she hadn't misled him out of spite or malice, but in an effort to keep barriers from growing up between them as she tried to get to know him better.

"Then what would you call it, Milly?" Rolfe asked tiredly. He rubbed his hand over his eyes and looked at her as if she were suddenly a total stranger.

I've been through this before, he thought with a pang of pain that lodged near his heart. He'd misjudged this woman, as he had Monique, and now he'd have to pay the price in bitter disillusionment.

"Rolfe, if it's the money, I can—"

"It's not a question of money, dammit!" Rolfe said fiercely.

"Then what is it? I don't understand what's wrong!" Her voice was growing shrill with desperation.

"What's wrong is more than a matter of dollars and cents. I'm not sure any longer what kind of woman you are."

"I'm no different from five minutes ago when you held me in your arms and made love to me—or have you forgotten that?" she demanded as fear sparked into anger.

"No, I haven't forgotten anything." He pushed his hands through his hair, then propped his elbows on his knees in a pensive posture.

"Then how can you say such a thing?"

"I don't know that I can love a woman who'd lie to me without batting an eyelash!"

"But Rolfe, I didn't lie to you!"

"You didn't tell me the truth, did you?"

"I didn't tell you about Carter Petroleum because you didn't need to know about it!" she said angrily. "I've never felt it to be anything but a burden, anyway!"

"Some burden," Rolfe replied, his voice laden with sarcasm. "How much would you say you're worth? Twenty million? Fifty?"

"It doesn't matter! Don't you understand?"

"It matters to me."

"What do you mean?"

"I mean I need some time to think things over, Milly. I spoke too soon about marriage."

"Oh, I see." A shaft of ice-cold agony impaled Milly's heart. She swallowed painfully, then stood up. She crossed her arms over her chest and held herself, shivering despite the heat in the attic.

"I have to be able to trust the woman I marry, and now I'm not sure . . ." Rolfe trailed off.

"Of course, I understand," she said bitterly. "Don't give it another thought. I guess there wasn't anything special between us anyway."

"Milly, I—" Rolfe's face was a solid, cold mask, but a muscle in his jaw jerked uncontrollably.

Milly's composure snapped. "Just get out, Rolfe! Get out!"

Her voice cracked, and she turned away, her fists clenched and her nails digging painfully into her palms as she struggled for control. She felt Rolfe pause, but she kept her shoulder turned stiffly from him. His steps echoed on the narrow staircase, then she was alone and desolate.

The journey from the transports of happiness to the depths of despair in such a few short minutes made Milly weak with reaction. A single burning tear scalded her cheek, then her anguished eyes brimmed over. Sliding to her knees beside the chaise, she buried her face in the worn fabric. She wept for the death of a stillborn dream, and her hot, bitter tears marked the green velvet like rain.

CHAPTER NINE

"Rolfe? Why are you sitting in the dark, son?" Amalie's worried voice interrupted Rolfe's black reverie. Amalie stood in the rectangle of Rolfe's front door. He rose stiffly from the armchair where he had been nursing his battered ego with the aid of a wineglass for the last several hours.

"Sorry, Mother," he muttered. "I didn't hear you drive up." He moved to turn on a lamp.

"I knew you wanted these financial statements in the morning, so I thought I'd save you a trip . . ." Amalie's words faltered as the golden glow of the lamp revealed her son's haggard face. "Something's the matter," she said with a mother's certainty. "What's happened?"

Rolfe grimaced and shrugged, then swallowed half the burgundy wine in his long-stemmed glass. "Nothing," he said, but his jaw was tight. His fingers idly twirled the glass and he stared at the fiery liquid in seeming fascination.

"Matthew Rolfe Hart! Answer me at once!" Amalie demanded, asserting her parental rights. The dark shadows under Rolfe's eyes alarmed her, and she had never seen him abuse a fine wine by throwing it to the back of his throat like so much rotgut whiskey.

"Mother, there are some things that even you can't fix," Rolfe said, his lips twisting.

"It's Milly, isn't it?" she demanded, moving into the circle of lamplight. She saw the flicker of pain behind Rolfe's eyes. It was at times like these that Amalie regretted Rolfe's ability to hide his feelings. He was so much like his father had been, polished and hard as a diamond on the outside, yet capable of deep inner feelings if tapped by the right woman. She felt a rising panic. She had grown to love Milly in the short time she had been here, and she had hoped . . . "What's happened to Milly?"

"I asked her to marry me."

"Is that all? It's about time! My goodness! You gave me such a shock," Amalie said, sinking onto the shabby sofa. "I thought something dreadful had happened!"

"You don't understand, Mother," Rolfe replied, his voice tight and strained. "She's been less than truthful about a lot of things. Marriage is out of the question now."

"You're going to have to explain better than that," his mother said, her voice crisp with exasperation. "Really, Rolfe, must you be so cryptic?"

Rolfe suddenly sat down beside her. "What if I told you she's worth millions, even though she lives like some kind of pauper?"

"I'd say I'm sure she had a good reason for not telling us," Amalie said, her voice calm.

"You'd like to believe that, wouldn't you? I guess I would, too. But owning a multimillion dollar corporation like Carter Petroleum is a bit much to just ignore. You think she's candid and without a trace of guile, but she's not really like that at all," he said bitterly.

Amalie watched Rolfe speculatively for a minute. "It's not the money, is it? It's the fact that she didn't tell you right away."

"I thought we had a relationship built on trust. She

151

looked at me with those big green eyes and I swallowed everything she said. When I found out the truth . . . Well, there's nothing left," he replied, his tone heavy. "I can't understand what reason she could have for doing such a thing."

"It's probably a very good one, to Milly's way of thinking," Amalie pointed out. Her lips lifted in a gentle smile. "You know she's something of an original. I'd give her the benefit of the doubt."

Rolfe jerked to his feet and slammed the crystal wineglass down on the coffee table so hard the delicate stem shattered.

"Damnation!" he said through gritted teeth. "She's hoodwinked you, too!"

"Calm down, Rolfe," Amalie ordered sharply. "You're overreacting, and if you'd stop just a moment you'd realize that Milly is not another Monique!"

"That's ancient history," Rolfe replied coldly. He dropped the remains of the broken glass. A piece rolled off the table, the crystal shards tinkling. Blood-red wine dripped silently to form a puddle on the floor. Trust his mother to put her finger on his most vulnerable spot. He thrust his hands through his hair in agitation.

"That history colors your perception of Milly!" Amalie protested. "What does it matter if she has money? We certainly aren't destitute ourselves, but I'll bet you never mentioned that last year's net was in six figures!"

"Yes, but that's different. She could see for herself—" Rolfe began.

Amalie gave a disgusted sigh and waved her manicured hand around the shabby room. "See from what? This? That expensive vehicle you drive? Your life-style doesn't exactly reflect your bank account either! If she's guilty, then so are you!"

"It's not that simple," Rolfe muttered.

"You were a stubborn little boy, too ready to hold a grudge, and you haven't changed one bit!" Amalie snapped. "Open your eyes! Milly's a lovely person. Whatever her resources, she works hard at a demanding career. She's been open and warm and honest about her *feelings,* and that's all that really counts. Why, everyone in Altus can tell you what an asset she is to this town! She's given so much of herself in such a short time, especially to Florie and Louella. And I know she cares for you, God help her. If you haven't got sense enough to see what's right in front of you, then you certainly don't deserve a woman like Milly!" Amalie grabbed her purse and stood, glaring up at her tall son. "Maybe she'd be better off without you, anyway!"

Rolfe stared as his mother slapped the bundle of papers down on the coffee table, then sailed regally out of the house. He had seldom seen her in such a temper, and could only gape after her. As the drone of her car faded into the quiet of the summer night, he dropped into the armchair and buried his face in his hands.

Was he being fair? Had Monique's betrayal destroyed his judgment and left him unable to trust? He rubbed his jaw and stared unseeingly at the blank, accusing eye of the television screen.

He had known from the first that Milly was a free spirit with a touch of the eccentric. Had his experience with Monique made him a coward, too scared to commit himself on faith alone? Milly had tried to explain, but he had ignored her, choosing to feed his wounded pride with a self-righteous indignation. Who, then, was more guilty?

Rolfe didn't know the answer. All he knew was that he loved Milly, wanted her desperately, and the thought of never seeing her again produced a gut-wrenching pain. She had said she loved him. What else really mattered? Nothing, he decided, his fist pounding into his cupped palm. He rose and crossed the room, ignoring the crunch of glass beneath his feet. He only hoped it wasn't too late.

Milly sat cross-legged on the rug in her apartment, listlessly separating the petals of Libby's crepe paper roses. The flowers were part of Libby's planned decorations for the masked ball, and Milly welcomed the mindless task. There was an all-encompassing ache in the region where once had been her heart, and she fought, without success, the feelings of betrayal and rejection. She tossed a completed stem into the growing pile beside her and reached for another colorful bud. Sebastian, sensing his mistress's mood, rested his chin on her thigh. His lop-ears drooped and he looked with sad, mournful eyes at Milly's preoccupied face.

Suddenly Sebastian's ears perked up, then he scrambled toward the front door, his claws tapping. A delighted yipping erupted from his throat as someone knocked. Milly answered the door still holding her flower.

"Hello, Milly," Rolfe said. After the afternoon's debacle, Milly had thought she'd never see him again, and shock registered on her face. "Could I talk to you?" Rolfe asked.

Milly's lungs refused to suck in air and her heart stopped, then slammed painfully against her rib cage. Her knuckles were white as she gripped the doorknob. He looked tired, she thought abstractedly, but his solemn face gave nothing away, as usual. Pain was replaced by a sudden thrust of white-hot rage. How dare he! How dare he come to her after what he had said! Hadn't she suffered enough?

"I don't have anything to say to you," she said through stiff lips. She began to push the door closed, but Rolfe's large hand caught it.

"Please, Milly."

"Haven't you said enough already?" she demanded, and was rewarded when he winced.

"I haven't said I'm sorry," he replied, swallowing hard. Milly jerked back as if she'd been struck.

"Go away," she whispered. She took a step backward, her jade green eyes wide and staring. Slowly Rolfe followed her into the apartment. "Don't do this to me, Rolfe," she pleaded. She grappled with the frayed edges of her composure, and her voice was a thin thread of sound.

"Please listen to me," Rolfe said gruffly. He reached for her, but she skittered away from his touch. Her feet trod through the pile of paper flowers and she reached down and scooped them up, holding them in front of her like a shield. Rolfe's hands dropped helplessly to his sides, and the muscle in his jaw twitched. "I was wrong this afternoon," he said hoarsely. "I know I hurt you. If I could take back each word, I would. I was confused and afraid . . . Milly, I'm so sorry. There's nothing I want more in this world than for you to marry me."

"I—I don't know if I can," she said, feeling as if she would choke on the words. He made a move toward her, but she backed away again, clutching her artificial bouquet tighter against her chest. "No, don't touch me! I can't think when you touch me."

"Then don't think," Rolfe growled, feeling goaded past endurance. He caught her in his strong arms and his mouth sought hers in a wordless apology. The flowers slipped unheeded from Milly's fingers as response washed through her in a wave, yet the hurt refused to dissolve completely. She clung to his shirt

155

front when he finally lifted his head. His breath warmed her temple. "I love you, honey. Nothing matters but that."

"But you didn't trust me," she said, trembling.

"It's not you," he protested. "When you hit me with your bombshell, I felt I'd been played for a fool again. Try to understand. It took me some hard thinking to realize the problem wasn't you, but me!" His voice was laden with self-disgust. "You're not Monique and never could be. If you'll give me another chance, I'll try to be worthy of *your* trust. I want to share my life with you."

"There are so many problems," she murmured brokenly. "And Carter Petroleum is only one of them."

"I don't think it's money itself that's a problem," Rolfe said slowly. "We can deal with the business aspects of your inheritance."

"It—it makes a difference no matter what I do," Milly said in a low voice. "I told you it was a burden. It's a barrier between me and the world. Look what it's done to us! I was afraid to tell you, afraid not to, so I did nothing and destroyed your faith in me. You say you understand, but what is it you really want, Rolfe? Me or Carter Petroleum?"

"That's a despicable accusation," Rolfe said heatedly.

"I know it is, but do you see *my* problem? Now how can I be sure about *you?*"

"By giving me your trust." Rolfe looked down at her and gave a faint, wry smile. "Don't worry that I'm marrying you for your money. The Hart Familie Vinery is having its best year ever. I should be able to support you in the manner to which you are accustomed."

"What?" Milly's fingers flew to her suddenly hot

156

cheeks. She struggled to readjust her thinking. "You mean you're not just a struggling businessman?"

"I'm struggling, all right—to make my winery the biggest in Arkansas!"

"I should have known there was money somewhere," Milly said, almost to herself. "Your polish, your confidence—I should have realized."

"You'll never have to worry about money," he assured her.

"Oh, Rolfe!" Milly's laugh was strangely mirthless. "How little you know about me! I've never had to worry about having too little, only too much!" She pulled out of his grasp and put a little distance between them.

"I've been doing some serious thinking, too. We're just too different for a permanent relationship ever to work."

"What are you saying?" Rolfe asked, feeling a sudden chill.

"Think about it! You're always logical, while I go strictly on instinct most of the time. We're always going in opposite directions."

"So we balance each other. It's a perfect compromise," Rolfe insisted.

"No, no! You've got to realize what it would mean. I know I'm impulsive and maybe more than a little naive. You think I'm cute or something, but what about in a few years? What kind of arguments would we have then?"

"The same as any couple. The type that makes kissing and making up very worthwhile." Rolfe's lips curved in a loving smile and he refused to be dissuaded.

"I'm serious, Rolfe!" Milly's voice rose with her frustration. "We'd be in trouble in no time! Everything

I do drives you crazy, and I can't be tied to a man who only tolerates me."

"Milly, I love you! Don't say that!"

"It's only the truth," Milly whispered, swallowing. "We can't let a—a physical infatuation blind us to reality. You're a fine man, but conventions are important to you, and I'm liable to be flaunting them at every opportunity. I need room to be who I am, and if I'm constantly worrying about injuring your dignity, then I'll only make us both miserable."

"Honey, I need you! I need your laughter, your sense of fun. It's the differences between us that drew us together in the first place!" Rolfe said.

Milly shook her head. "No, Rolfe. I'd end up making you terribly unhappy, and I couldn't stand that. I don't want to be the one who earns your hate." Her voice cracked. "I can't help the way I am, any more than you can help who you are. Let's not break each other's hearts."

"You really mean it, don't you?" he asked, suddenly weighed down by feelings of desperation and helplessness. How could he convince her she was totally wrong? "We have something very special, Milly. When you're in my arms, I've never felt anything so wonderful, so right. We can't just walk away from that."

"It's just physical," she denied, but her traitorous body quivered with tantalizing memories. Rolfe's hand was warm on her forearm as he pulled her gently to him.

"Liar. It was more than that for both of us, and you know it!" he said firmly. "I don't care how many obstacles you throw up, because we're meant to be together! I'll prove it to you somehow! I'm not giving up." His lips covered hers in a sensual refutation of her words, then he released her.

She swayed on her feet. "You'd just be wasting your time," Milly whispered, near tears.

Rolfe strode to the door, then turned and surveyed her trembling form, his eyes narrowed slightly at the response she could not deny. Suddenly his expression relaxed, and he gave a confident smile.

"We'll see about that," he promised softly. Then he disappeared into the night.

"I really appreciate your helping out," Ben Rollins said several days later as they stood near the front door of the Altus *Spectator.*

"I don't mind at all," Milly replied. "Is Libby feeling any better?"

Ben groaned and shook his head. "Not much. Nobody told me this baby business could be so rough! If she's not asleep, she's sick!"

"I'm sure it will pass in time," Milly said comfortingly. "In the meantime, my apartment is full of paper flowers, the arrangements for refreshments for the dance have been made, and here's Libby's announcement for the paper."

Ben accepted the typewritten paper and dropped a kiss of gratitude on Milly's cheek. "With your help, we just may get through this year's Grape Festival with our sanity intact!"

Milly knew that the festival would begin in a few days' time. Already there was an air of anticipation running through the little town. Between inventorying the Abington house and working with Libby on the masked ball, Milly had managed to stay quite busy. She hadn't seen Rolfe, despite his promise to the contrary, and she didn't know whether she was disappointed or relieved. She was pledged to stay in Altus at least until after this weekend's masked ball. Since she doubted seriously if the Abington sisters would allow her to sell any of their possessions, there was little point in remaining in town after the survey was completed. It was nearly done now, but somehow she hadn't yet been able to face returning to the attic. It was something she'd have to do soon, but no matter how often she lectured herself, she knew that it would be a very long time indeed before she recovered from Rolfe Hart.

"Rolfe is escorting you to the dance, isn't he?" Ben asked now.

"No," Milly admitted, shaking her dark head. She sighed. As Rolfe's best friend, she guessed Ben had a right to know. "We're not seeing each other again."

"What!" Ben exclaimed. "That's the dumbest thing I've ever heard. He's obviously crazy about you! I'll just give him my two cents' worth the next time I see him!"

"Don't, Ben," Milly said. "It's not Rolfe, it's me," she admitted.

Ben's expression was totally dumbfounded for a second. Suddenly a loud droning noise filled the air.

"What the hell is that?" Ben asked, craning his neck to peer out the plate glass window. Milly's small smile was humorless. It was certain that Ben was glad to change the subject. The droning grew louder as Ben pushed open the glass door and they stepped out onto the sidewalk. "Where's it coming from?" Ben said, shading his eyes against the glare of the afternoon sun.

"Over there," Milly said, pointing a slim finger toward the horizon. "What's that?"

"It looks like a—holy cow! Where's my camera?" Ben dashed into the newspaper office and returned in a flash. While he fumbled with the settings, Milly studied the strangest-looking flying contraption she had ever seen! Darting like an oversize dragonfly, the machine's fragile metal skeleton glinted brightly in the brilliant sunshine. The roaring of its engine increased to a deafening level, then the aircraft lost altitude suddenly. Milly gasped as it dipped sharply, then leveled out a mere twenty feet above the main street and buzzed the town.

"What is that?" Milly gasped.

"Ultralight helicopter," Ben explained. "Look, he's pulling something behind." Milly squinted to spell out the letters of the message on the long banner floating behind the 'copter.

"A-l-t-u-s, Altus! Attend Altus Grape Festival!" she read, laughing. "That's great! Ben, was this your idea?"

Ben's wide mouth curved into a grin. "Wish it was! But I can't take credit for that! Oops! Get ready to duck, here he comes!" The 'copter flashed over them with a loud chop-chop-chop.

"Who's flying that thing?" Milly asked. The entire town was now out on the streets, laughing and pointing at the antics of this flying clown.

"I don't know, but he was wearing some sort of purple getup." Ben laughed, snapping the camera rapidly. "Here he comes again!"

This time Milly got a clear, if brief, view of the pilot of the strange helicopter as he again dive-bombed the town street with his colorful banner. "He's wearing a mask, too!" she exclaimed, jumping up and down with excitement. "Isn't this great? Altus has its own superhero! Just like Spiderman, or the Scarlet Pimpernel!"

"We'll call him the—the Purple Avenger!" Ben cried excitedly. The camera clicked madly. "We'll have all of northern Arkansas come to our Grape Festival to see the Purple Avenger! But who is that guy?"

That was the question everyone continued to ask during the next few days. Not only had the Purple

Avenger taken the town by storm, capturing everyone's imagination, but his arrival was coupled with the strangest series of events that Altus had ever seen.

First, it was the mysterious appearance of bright purple ribbons all over town that had everyone talking. Overnight they were festooned on signposts, tied around trees, and decorating the doors of all the public buildings. Then they began appearing in more unlikely places, like grocery carts, bicycles, and finally Milly's jeep!

Fleeting glimpses of the Purple Avenger had people constantly on the lookout for the elusive individual. He was seen at a high school assembly, then nonchalantly standing with a bunch of dignitaries at a groundbreaking. Once he even rode through the middle of town on a purple motorcycle, his purple cape flying behind him, but everyone was too stunned to mount a chase before the Purple Avenger rode off into the proverbial sunset.

Many a feminine heart throbbed at the attractive male body revealed by the tight purple stockings and form-fitting suit.

As Festival day approached, the excitement began to get out of hand, and although many things were blamed on the Purple Avenger, Milly had the feeling that people were using the mystery man as an excuse for madness. Practical jokes of all descriptions were played continually, and Ben had a hard time reporting them all in the *Spectator*. Television crews from neighboring cities swarmed over the little town, much to Ben's delight, and the upcoming Grape Festival was heavily publicized.

Milly received enigmatic notes in the mail written in purple ink, and the florist shop had orders to deliver her a purple carnation daily. She didn't quite know what to think about all this, but it touched a responsive chord in her zany personality. Whoever was running this thing had her admiration! The comical goings-on helped take her mind off Rolfe, at least for a bit.

Small, puzzling gifts wrapped in purple paper and ribbons were delivered to the principal organizers of the festival, and Milly was included with a violet silk nosegay, lavender soap, and a plush purple velveteen dog that had a remarkable resemblance to Sebastian. She was showing Florie her latest acquisition the day before the festival when Louella stormed into the house.

"That infuriating man!" Louella muttered, her lips compressed in a thin line and her faded brown eyes sparkling with outrage. Milly had never seen her so upset.

"What is it?" Florie asked in alarm.

Louella sank down onto the worn love seat and began to peel off her gloves. "It's disaster, that's what it is!" Louella snapped. "I just saw Mr. Jenkins at the bank. They're going to foreclose on us, Florie!"

"What? Oh, it can't be, Lulu! Whatever are we going to do?" Florie wrung her hands in agitation.

"Surely you can work something out," Milly began anxiously.

"It's impossible! Mr. Jenkins mentioned filing"— Louella caught her breath and shuddered—"bankruptcy."

"Oh, the disgrace!" Florie cried. Her eyes overflowed, and tears streamed down her wrinkled cheeks.

"Exactly." Louella seemed to pull herself together. "This is clearly no time for sentiment. Papa would turn over in his grave at the thought! Well, no Abington has ever gone into bankruptcy, and neither will we! We'll just have to sell the house. Milly, do you think you could dispose of that furniture? Start with the mahogany whatnot."

"Oh, but Louella, what will you do?" Milly began.

"This is no time for nonsense, Milly," Louella replied, her mouth pursed over this distasteful task. "We'll work something out, but first we must settle our debts. How much could you get for all the furniture?"

"I'm not sure, but much less if we have to rush the sale than if I could market it selectively," Milly said.

"There's no time for that. I guess we'll just have to take Mr. Singleton up on his offer."

"Not him!" Florie cried, beginning to sob in earnest.

"Wait, Louella," Milly said desperately. "I have some money. Let me help you."

"No, dear, we couldn't possibly," Louella replied, patting Milly's hand kindly. "You're so sweet to offer and we appreciate it, but it's time Florie and I faced facts."

Florie made a visible effort to control her weeping, then threw herself into her sister's arms and hugged her.

"You're right, of course, Lulu," Florie said, swallowing hard. "I'll just go talk to Buford about this."

"You shouldn't be too hasty," Milly said, thinking furiously. "Look, the festival is tomorrow, and everyone will be too busy to think straight. Promise me that you'll delay your decision until afterward. That's the only smart thing to do."

"I suppose you're right about that." Louella sighed. She looked at her sister, then her gaze roamed over the shabby but homey room. "We might as well enjoy ourselves while we can."

"Good," Milly said, relaxing a bit. "Something will turn up; you'll see."

The sisters disappeared to their rooms to compose

their feelings, and Milly headed immediately for the telephone in the hall. She got through to Gareth with a minimum of difficulty, then explained the situation succinctly and ordered him to make an offer to the bank for the purchase of the Abington house. Although Gareth was curious, he knew better than to question Milly when her mind was made up. He promised to see to it immediately and told Milly he'd call her back.

Milly turned away from the phone still clutching her silly purple puppy, a pensive expression on her face. She stopped short when she saw Rolfe standing at the end of the hall.

"How long have you been standing there eavesdropping?" she demanded, the sudden surge of longing making her voice harsh.

"Long enough to know the ladies are in trouble," he said quietly. The sunshine streaming in from the rear porch threw his silhouette into relief in the dim hall. "Is Gareth the lawyer you talked about?"

Milly jerked, and her hands tightened on the toy dog. "Yes. If you'll excuse me, I've got to go help Libby with the decorations for the dance." She moved stiffly past him, but Rolfe's large warm hand captured her elbow to stop her.

"Milly, I know you're trying to help the ladies, but it's not necessary, really," he said gently.

"I'll be the judge of that!" she snapped. "What are you doing here, anyway?"

"Do you have to ask?" Rolfe's lean face was solemn, and his jaw clenched. The pressure of his hand changed subtly and became a caress. "I've tried to give you some space, but I couldn't stop wanting you!"

Milly closed her eyes and shivered violently. "Rolfe, please," she whispered, swaying. "Don't make it harder than it is."

"You're being stubborn, Milly," Rolfe said. His hands clasped her shoulders and gently pulled her toward him until his breath touched her hair. "I want you and I love you. If you've got any courage at all, you'll admit you feel the same."

"It doesn't change anything," Milly said desperately. "I can tell you all day long I love you, that you're sexy and sensitive and a thousand other admirable things, but I'm still not right for you! I'm the loony-tune, the wacko, remember? And you're an upright and solid citizen, and so annoyingly straitlaced! It would never work!"

"We could make it work," he murmured. "I'll prove it to you." His lips brushed hers, and Milly couldn't prevent the stifled moan of pleasure and need that stole from her throat. That was all the encouragement Rolfe needed. His mouth slanted over hers hungrily in a sensual persuasion that threatened the foundations of Milly's hard-won decision. With a supreme effort, she wrenched herself free.

"You can make me forget, but that's not proof!" she said, her breath rasping painfully. "There's no way you can convince me, Rolfe, so please—please don't try anymore. It hurts too much." Her voice dropped to a whisper, and her green eyes were full of pain. Then she turned and practically ran out of the house.

Rolfe bent and picked up the forgotten purple toy she had dropped. A frown pleated his brow, and his jaw clenched with misery.

"Well, pup," he murmured, gazing after Milly's retreating figure, "I guess we'll see soon enough if I can change her mind."

The day of the Altus Grape Festival dawned hot and sunny, but Milly's thoughts were gloomy. An early morning call from Gareth informed her that he had failed in his mission. The officials at the bank had told him that a previous offer had been made and was in the process of being accepted. It looked as though obnoxious Dean Singleton had beaten them all to the punch and would succeed in his plans to transform the Abington home into some kind of tacky tourist trap! Milly was devastated, but strove to conceal her feelings from the sisters. If they had made a decision despite her pleas to wait, then she would have to abide by it.

Milly, Louella, and Florie all wore expressions of determined cheerfulness when they gathered to drive to the Altus City Park, where the festival was to be held. Even Buford had shed his normal morose attitude, as well as his dungarees. He looked quite spiffy in a crisp starched shirt and bright red bow tie as he helped Florie with the jars of grape jelly she intended to enter in one of the contests.

Once they arrived at the tree-shaded park, it didn't take long for them to join in the spirit of fun that pervaded the area. A large crowd had already gathered and applauded enthusiastically when Ben announced the official opening of the festival from the grandstand.

"It's a good crowd, isn't it?" Libby asked excitedly, coming up beside Milly. She was dressed similarly to Milly, in shorts and sneakers, but she sported a bright purple T-shirt with the inscription Altus Grape Festival.

"Great. Are you feeling okay?" Milly questioned as other dignitaries made their official welcome.

"Just fine. Besides, I wouldn't have missed this for the world! Look!"

"Oh, my God!" Milly laughed. At that moment a large white horse appeared around the corner of the square. The rider, dressed in the now-familiar form-

167

fitting purple costume, held an enormous bunch of purple and lavender balloons. As the masked individual galloped around the park, he loosed the balloons, and children and their parents as well began a mad scramble to capture the floating globes.

"The Purple Avenger strikes again!" Libby chortled.

"That man's a nut!" Milly laughed, straining on tiptoe to see over the crowd. All she got was a fleeting glimpse of the Avenger as he disappeared as suddenly as he had come. "Come clean, Libby. Who is that guy?"

"I swear I don't know." Libby giggled. "Ben got a note to expect something unusual, but that was too much! It's certainly put everyone in a festive mood. As hard as we've worked, we deserve some fun. Let's go enter the contests. Are you game?"

"Sure!" Milly agreed enthusiastically.

She and Libby were soon caught up in the general excitement. They became contestants in the grape-in-a-spoon race, then tried their luck in the grape-seed-spitting contest. What they lacked in distance and accuracy, they made up for in enthusiasm.

"Having fun?"

Milly looked away from Libby's attempt at seed spitting at the sound of Rolfe's question. He had joined her on the sidelines of the event without her noticing. He was faintly flushed under his tan, and his blond hair was damp with perspiration from the hot sun. He looked virile and extremely masculine in his festival T-shirt and shorts, and Milly's heart ached.

"Lots of fun," she murmured. She tried desperately to think of a safe topic of conversation. "Are you going to give it a try?"

"Sure. Why not?" he said, surprising her. She would once have thought Rolfe too concerned about his dignity to join in such an outlandish exhibition. A roar of approval went up around them. "Will you look at that? Libby's in the lead!"

Libby bounced over to where they stood, and they offered their congratulations. After that it seemed natural for Rolfe to walk around with them. It was a painful sort of pleasure for Milly, but she was loath to abandon it. They cheered for each other as they tried the grape vault, a contest to see how high a person could toss a grape and catch it in his or her mouth. Milly posted a good score, but they meandered away before they learned the final results.

Rolfe admired the two women and offered suggestions as they had small designs painted on their cheeks at the face-painting booth. Then they all gathered at the tug-of-war pit to scream encouragement to the teams joined in the struggle for a trophy. Both Milly and Libby decided to pass as the snake rodeo was announced, but Rolfe went to watch while the women admired the displays of jelly and fresh-picked grapes. Booths sponsored by the Hart, Post and Wiederkehr wineries offered samples of their best vintages and free tours, but Milly kept her distance, remembering with chagrin how much damage those "little cups" could do!

Ben joined them later in the afternoon as they picnicked under the shade trees on treats purchased from the various food booths. The crowd was beginning to thin, but Milly couldn't remember when she had enjoyed a day more. Despite an initial reluctance to be in Rolfe's company, Milly had succumbed to his charm and undemanding companionship. She stored up memories for a future without him, basking in his presence and ignoring the pain in her heart. She knew that she was doing what was best for both of them, but she was human enough to cling to these precious moments with him.

Ben excused himself to go announce the winners of the various competitions, so Milly, Libby, and Rolfe gathered around the grandstand to listen. Suddenly Milly stiffened.

"What is it?" Rolfe asked, sensitive to her mood.

"Mr. Singleton. He's watching us," Milly muttered.

Rolfe glanced up to see Dean grinning maliciously at Milly from several feet away. His expression became instantly bland when he saw Rolfe's attention focus on him.

"Don't worry about him," Rolfe advised, glancing back at Milly. She had turned slightly away from Dean's unnerving stare and tried to brush off her unease.

"I won't, but I don't like him. And I think the Abington sisters are being forced to sell to him."

"You mustn't worry about that," Rolfe began, but he was interrupted by the applause of the crowd as Ben announced Libby's name as winner of the women's seed spitting competition! Ben continued to grin widely as his petite wife bounced up on the grandstand to receive her award. Then he called Milly's name as the winner in the grape vault.

"Go ahead, that's you," Rolfe encouraged with a proud grin, sending Milly blushing with pleasure up to the grandstand. By the time the awards had all been announced, Florie had also won two first places and a second for her grape jellies, and a smiling Buford gallantly escorted her to the stage to receive her ribbons. He pleased the assembled spectators greatly when he "saluted her cheek" with a kiss of congratulation, then led a flustered and blushing Florie away.

The tired but happy crowd began to disperse after

the final announcements, but Ben called Milly back to the stage.

"There's a box up here for you," he said. Milly curiously accepted the large square box sloppily wrapped in an identifying purple paper. An unfamiliar handwriting addressed the box to her. Libby sat down on the edge of the grandstand as Rolfe and Ben watched. A few curious onlookers, including Dean Singleton, waited nearby.

"Well, go ahead, open it," Libby demanded, the perky butterfly painted on her cheek making her look like a flower child.

"It feels kind of strange," Milly said, shaking the mysterious package.

"The Purple Avenger again!" Ben guessed.

Rolfe frowned thoughtfully as Milly tugged the paper from the box and lifted the lid. What she saw made her scream and slam the lid back on the box.

"What is it?" Rolfe demanded urgently.

"Ugh! It's snakes!" Milly said, shuddering and dropping the box on the edge of the grandstand. "Somebody's got a warped sense of humor!"

"What?" Ben cried. He and Rolfe inspected the box's contents as Milly and Libby backed away in disgust. "Well, I'll be damned! It's the contestants from the snake rodeo! How'd they get in here?"

"I don't care how, but I think I know who!" Milly said. She spotted Dean Singleton's ruddy face on the edge of the crowd and suddenly knew without a doubt who had engineered this repulsive practical joke!

"Hey, you! Wait a minute!" she shouted.

Dean turned on his heel at her shout, instantly acknowledging his guilt. Milly caught up with him in a flash, then shook her finger in his face. "And another thing, you obnoxious jerk!"

Rolfe intervened, suddenly clenching his large hand

171

in Dean's shirt front. "Control yourself, Milly," he said, his voice mild. "There's no need to get so worked up over a little joke. After all, Dean did make quite a contribution to the historical society."

"That—that's what I thought, Rolfe," Dean said weakly. "No harm done."

"Rolfe, you traitor!" Milly stormed. "I can take a joke, but this—this twerp is going to turn the Abington estate into God knows what kind of dump, so don't you take his side!"

"Now, Milly," Rolfe said, his voice silky, "I'm sure Dean is going to apologize. Aren't you, Dean?" Rolfe shook Dean by the shirt front, nearly lifting him from his shoes.

"I—I—I—" Dean stuttered comically.

"After all," Rolfe continued, "he understands now how important you are to me. Don't you, Dean?"

Another shake.

"And if he ever tried anything like this again, he realizes I would be forced to defend the woman I love. Don't you, Dean?"

Another shake.

Dean's head bobbled and his mouth opened and closed like a gasping fish. Milly realized suddenly that Rolfe was in a controlled yet furious rage. She drew an alarmed gasp.

"Let him go, Rolfe," she said.

"Don't worry, love," Rolfe said softly. "I'm not going to hit him." The blue of his eyes blanched icy cold. "The hell I'm not!"

Milly gave a little squeal of horror and she caught Rolfe's free arm with her two hands. Dean threw his hands over his face and whimpered.

"Rolfe! Please, let him go!" She dangled from his arm like a rag doll.

Rolfe glanced at her, his mouth twisting as he deliberated. "You sure, Milly?" he asked.

"Sure I'm sure!" Milly yelped desperately. Rolfe studied her for a moment, then unclenched his fist from Dean's shirt. Milly loosened her grip on his arm with a sigh of relief.

"I try to give the lady everything she wants, Dean," Rolfe said conversationally. "Why don't you just get the hell out of here?"

"Yeah, sorry! Won't ever happen again," Dean babbled. He backed away cautiously, then turned and scampered out of the park.

"Mercy!" Libby sighed. "I thought you were gonna flatten him for sure!"

"Hmm, me, too," Rolfe admitted, flexing his hand in mild astonishment. "I sounded like John Wayne telling him not to mess with my woman!"

"Agggh!" Three pairs of eyes turned at Milly's frustrated cry. "Good God! Now look what I've made you do!"

"What's the matter?" Rolfe asked. "Didn't you want me to take up for you? I thought you'd be pleased I could discard my so-called dignity long enough to come to your rescue!"

"I'm not the Lone Ranger and you're not John Wayne!" Milly raved. "You'd never have acted like that except for me! It's all my fault! I'm not a good influence on you! Oh, Rolfe," she moaned. "I was right! I've got to get out of your life before I do any more damage!" With that she burst into tears and hurried away.

Rolfe watched her in open-mouthed wonder.

"What was that all about?" Ben demanded.

"The hell if I know," Rolfe growled. "I've got to find some way to marry that nutty woman before she drives me totally insane!"

173

CHAPTER TEN

"Oh, but Libby, I couldn't! Not after today!" Milly wailed.

"Nonsense," Libby replied. "After all the work you've done on this masked ball, there's no way I'm going to allow you to miss it!"

Milly felt a sinking sensation. Things were rapidly going from bad to worse! After her outburst at the festival all she wanted to do was sink into a hole and die, but Libby was adamant. They had driven back to the Abington house with Louella and Florie and now stood on the front steps. Although Milly realized that Libby probably thought she was doing her friend a favor, Milly knew that she didn't want to face anyone in public, especially Rolfe. Milly searched desperately for any excuse.

"I don't have a costume, anyway," she said lamely.

"There ought to be something suitable packed away in the attic," Louella offered helpfully. "And I agree with Libby; you certainly must attend. Why, what if Libby starts to feel poorly? Who'll take over?"

"That's right, Milly," Libby agreed. "I need you to be there."

Milly hesitated and felt herself weakening. She was helpless to resist an appeal of that nature. "But Louella, you and I and Florie need to talk about your selling the house," she protested feebly.

"Never mind that tonight," Louella said with a dismissive wave. She moved toward the front door. "I'm too tired. Tomorrow will be soon enough to discuss our decision."

"Lulu's right," Florie said. "Besides, I'll have to hurry if I'm to be ready when Buford comes to pick me up. We certainly aren't going to miss this ball, and you shouldn't either!"

"Oh, all right," Milly decided. What further harm could it do? She was already in the most miserable state she had ever been in. Nothing could make her feel any worse.

"Now you're talking!" Libby exclaimed. "Ben and I will pick you up. See you later!"

But Milly was wrong. She felt much worse when she climbed into the attic in search of a costume and saw the lovely Victorian wedding gown draped across the wire dress form. Sitting on an old trunk, she stared at the dress for a long time, her emotions so confused that she was sure only of the anguish she felt.

What do I really want? she asked herself forlornly. For a brief time today she and Rolfe had enjoyed each other's company, and she had almost believed they could find a way to make their relationship work. The sensual spark was still there, waiting to flame into life. But they were too different. She'd have to come to grips with that reality—and fast. But did it have to hurt so much? You'll get over him, she told herself, and knew that she lied. The only thing to do was get out of Altus as fast as she could. Maybe that would be possible after tomorrow. Reluctantly she began to look through the trunk for a costume. Somehow she had to get through tonight first.

Milly's mood lightened a bit when Ben and Libby picked her up that evening. She laughed out loud when a perky redhead in a red gingham dress popped out of the station wagon driven by a turbaned individual.

"Oh, my goodness! It's Little Orphan Annie and Punjab!" she said with a laugh.

"At your service, memsahib." Ben grinned as she climbed into the car.

"That's a super flapper costume," Libby complimented. Milly's simple shift dress was an authentic twenties design, covered from its scooped neckline to its high hem with jet bugle beads that swished seductively when she moved. "Are you supposed to be anybody special?" Milly adjusted the unusual black feathered half-mask, then dramatically tossed her black ostrich boa around her throat.

"I beg your pardon," she said haughtily. "Haven't you ever heard of Hard-hearted Hanna, the Vamp of Savannah?"

"You'll knock 'em dead, honey." Ben grinned as he drove. "Watch out for falling bodies, especially Rolfe's!"

Milly stiffened. "Is Rolfe coming?" she asked in a small voice.

"Sure, but he didn't say as what, did he?" Libby replied curiously.

"Probably something exciting, like an accountant or a banker." Ben laughed. "He told me before that costume parties just aren't his thing."

Milly felt her throat thicken and her eyes sting at the thought of seeing Rolfe. She knew that this evening was destined to be sheer torture and prayed that it would soon be over.

But once they arrived, Milly was too busy helping Libby with the final arrangements to dwell on her unhappy thoughts. They set out refreshments in Rolfe's nearly unrecognizable shed, transformed for tonight with arbors of paper roses and dozens of green ferns. Tables and chairs along one wall offered seating for weary dancers, and the warm night air was sweet and fragrant as it wafted through the wide open doors. Candles in hurricane globes softly illuminated the scene as the band tuned up in one corner.

People began to arrive, dressed in costumes ranging from the predictable to the outrageous. Milly had to rush to congratulate Florie and Buford when they arrived as Laurel and Hardy. Soon a crush of people crowded the dance floor. It was decidedly amusing to watch a dill pickle waltzing with the Wicked Witch of the West. Milly danced several times with Ben and a few other men friends who sat at the Rollins's table, but there was no sign of Rolfe. As the night wore on, Milly's misery increased in direct proportion to the rising gaiety of the jolly crowd. At last she could stand it no longer and went in search of a little solitude.

She dreaded seeing Rolfe, for her love had not diminished, and she feared she would give in if he pressed his case again. So why, then, was she so disappointed that he hadn't come at all? Did that mean he had finally given up? Strangely, there was no sense of relief in that thought.

The happy throng filled every inch of the shed and even spilled outside into the starlight night. Milly moved through the crowd, which seemed to be made up only of happy couples, until she at last found a quiet area outside on the far side of the shed nearest the rows of grape vines. She could hear the faint melody of a love song from inside and sighed. She rested against the cool steel siding of the shed, her head back and her eyes closed, as she tried to become one with the soothing peacefulness of the night. Somehow she had to ease the ache in her heart or it would surely destroy her soul.

"Pretty bird, are you the one I've been looking for?" a deep voice asked beside Milly's ear. She gave a faint gasp and opened her eyes, but she could only make out the dark shadow of a tall form blocking the starlight.

"I don't know," she answered faintly. Her shoulders pressed harder against the shed wall as the shadow loomed closer. "Who do you want?"

"You," he murmured.

Milly felt warm breath stir the feathers of her mask and the artful tendrils of her hairdo. A quiver passed through her at the deep, seductive timbre of his one-word answer. A split second of panic invaded Milly's consciousness. The darkness, the solid outline of the stranger, the unveiled need in his tone frightened her, but before she could put a voice to her fear his mouth covered hers, warm, seeking, and irresistibly familiar. Her lips quivered in a tiny smile of recognition. She would know Rolfe anywhere.

"It's you," she breathed against his lips in relief. Gone were any thoughts of protest. It was enough for the moment that she was with him.

"Who am I?" he asked, moving even closer. His hands pressed against the wall next to Milly's shoulders, trapping her. Milly's eyelashes fanned down, and her lips parted in subtle invitation.

"It doesn't matter," she whispered. An unbearable excitement began to build as an erotic fantasy took life in the darkness. Lips nibbled the shell of her ear, sending delicious shivers down Milly's spine, and he inhaled her delicate scent as if it were an elixir necessary to life. His mouth trailed across her cheek, then brushed her lips lightly.

"How can you be so sure?" he asked, and his voice betrayed a secret amusement. His hands clasped her shoulders, pulling her around so that the starlight fell full on his face—a face concealed by the tight hood of the Purple Avenger!

Milly gasped aloud, but before she could react, before she could even wonder, he captured her mouth, plundering the hidden sweetness with his tongue until she quivered helplessly against him, her knees like jelly and her brain numb to everything except the sensual pleasure of his kiss. Clasped tightly to him, she could feel the heat of his body through the tight knit of his costume, and her fingers tangled in the fullness of his flamboyant cape.

"Beware the night, pretty bird, or you'll find your favors stolen by a rogue," he warned, laughing softly, then he released her. He whirled away with a flip of his cape while Milly swayed in a dizzy circle, and his mocking laughter floated on the warm night air.

Milly came down to earth with a jolt. "Wait!" she cried, her stumbling feet sabotaging her efforts to follow him. "Rolfe? You—come back!" She shook her head in disbelief. The Purple Avenger was *Rolfe? Her* Rolfe had crammed his body into those revealing purple tights and pulled all those outlandish stunts? No, it couldn't be! He wouldn't ever do a thing like that! But then that meant a total stranger had kissed her intimately, stirring her to passion in the fleeting heat of a moment! Her cheeks burned and her breath puffed erratically from her lungs in a tortured wheeze. She had to know for sure—she had to!

A shadow turned the corner of the building, and Milly followed him, her feet flying. The voluminous purple cape billowed outward as the Purple Avenger dashed into the crowded interior of the shed, disappearing into the midst of the dancing throng.

Milly pushed into the crowd after him. "Stop him! It's the Purple Avenger!" she shouted, desperately pushing between the dancers. She caught a fleeting glimpse of a purple-cowled head moving across the room. "Don't let him get away!" she cried.

Confusion grew within the crowd, surprised faces becoming eager as the Purple Avenger was recognized and the dancers took up the cry. Milly pushed free of the last obstacle just as the Purple Avenger ran out the large back door of the shed.

"There he goes!" she shouted. "Don't let him get away!"

She ran out the door, followed by a zany assemblage eager to track down the elusive hero of the Grape Festival. Dogs and dancers, princesses and pachyderms, nursery rhyme characters and rock 'n' roll stars all took up the chase. It was a giant, loony game of follow-the-leader and even the band forsook its medley of forties hits to swing into a rousing Sousa march!

The Purple Avenger disappeared down a row of grape vines. Milly's feather boa streamed out behind her as she ran after him. She cursed her high heels, stopping for a moment to remove them, then sprinting down the plowed row in hot pursuit, with the costumed menagerie right behind her. To her chagrin, her quarry seemed to vanish into thin air!

"There he goes!" shouted a voice.

Milly paused, then noticed a movement several rows over. She ducked under the wires of the grape arbor, brushed through the wide, tough leaves, and glanced up and down each row until she again caught sight of the Avenger loping quietly back in the direction of the shed.

He was trying to double back! She scurried down the adjacent row, holding her shoes one in each hand, her bare feet scuffling through the loose earth. Behind her costumed characters bobbed in and out among the leafy grape vines in a macabre starlight dance. Milly

180

and the Avenger reached the end of their respective rows almost at the same time.

"Hold it, you!" Milly yelled, flinging one shoe at her quarry.

"After him!" a voice Milly recognized as Ben's shouted gleefully. The Purple Avenger gave a grunt as Milly's shoe struck him on his broad back, but he merely laughed and jogged a bit faster. Infuriated, Milly launched her other shoe, which sailed harmlessly over his head, then plunged after him, racing between the abandoned grape hoppers and wagons. The shouts of the other runners sounded closer. She was winded and panting but refused to give up, so when the Purple Avenger made his final dash out past the last wagon, heading for the parking lot, Milly knew it was then or never.

With a spurt of adrenaline-produced energy, she let out a blood-curdling scream that jerked her prey into momentary hesitation, just long enough for Milly to launch the prettiest flying tackle a pro football coach would ever hope to see. She hit him just above the knees, and they both went down in a cloud of dust, rolling over and over under the force of the impact. Milly ended up on top.

"Got you now!" she panted, her fingers digging into the purple knit of his costume. Her mask was long gone, her hair fell down about her shoulders, and she was covered with a layer of dirt, but she was triumphant.

People crowded in on all sides of them.

"Who is it?"

"Take off his mask!"

Strong hands shifted Milly so that they were both sitting up, and the sound of deep laughter issued from the downed Avenger.

"Well, woman, do you intend to make a habit of this?" he asked merrily, helping Milly to her feet.

Milly gasped. Those blue eyes behind that purple cowl could only belong to one man. She reached up and began to peel off the mask.

"Look this way, Milly!" Ben called, the flash of his camera making fireworks in the darkness. Milly was too intent on tugging the cowl off the Avenger's head to pay any attention. With a jerk, the cowl slipped off. The assembled crowd gasped, then murmured and began to cheer as Rolfe's grinning face was revealed.

Milly stared, open-mouthed and speechless, and dropped the mask to the ground. Rolfe ruffled the hair plastered to his forehead, and his mouth quirked mischievously. The cheering increased when he suddenly caught Milly's nape in one hand, then proceeded to kiss her thoroughly.

"Rolfe?" she gasped, still disbelieving, when he lifted his head. His arm curved around her waist in support. His face was flushed, and his grin was young and boyish.

"Man, you're the greatest!" Ben exclaimed, shaking his friend's hand enthusiastically. "You had us all going! Who'd have ever thought?" He shot several more pictures as others in the crowd added their congratulations.

Milly's amazement was complete. She could not get over the fact that dignified, sometimes even pompous Rolfe had made such a spectacle of himself before the entire town! It was so totally unbelievable that her mind rebelled. She stared up at Rolfe, who was laughing and obviously enjoying his role as mastermind of the biggest practical joke ever played in Altus. It was too much to grasp all at once.

"What do you say, honey?" Rolfe asked finally, giving Milly's shoulder a squeeze. "Did I have you fooled, too?" The crowd around them had cleared away, the merrymakers returning to the enticing strains of music inside the shed now that the excitement was over.

"I still can't believe this," Milly said faintly.

"Come on, you two," Ben said, indicating the shed with a grin. "The party's just begun!"

"I think Milly needs a few minutes to collect herself," Rolfe said dryly, amused by the dazed look in Milly's green eyes. He quirked an eyebrow at Ben, and his friend shrugged and gave him a wink. Then Ben grabbed Libby's hand and followed the crowd back inside. Rolfe's arm silently urged Milly forward, and they began to walk away from the noise and gaiety of the ball. The warm serenity of the night enveloped them as they headed down the road toward the dim outline of Rolfe's house.

"Why?" Milly asked, her voice breathless. Barefoot, she picked her way gingerly, clinging to the support of Rolfe's arm, but she was oblivious to everything except her all-consuming astonishment.

"Don't you know?" he questioned softly.

Milly shook her head helplessly. "I can't imagine."

Rolfe drew a deep breath and continued to walk, his gaze directed to the starlit heavens. Had all his efforts been for nothing? Couldn't she see?

"Can you imagine how I felt when you told me I was too solid and upright for you? What better way to prove to you once and for all that I love you just the way you are? And if life with you takes a zany course occasionally, I'll be right there at your side."

"You did it for me?" Her voice was unbelieving. They had walked as far as Rolfe's house and now paused at the bottom of the porch steps.

"I need you, Milly. You've taught me to laugh again

and opened my heart. I can't imagine living my life without you now."

"Are you sure?" she whispered.

"How can you tell a man he's too serious for you when he's wearing purple tights?" Rolfe asked.

Suddenly Milly began to laugh. A feeling of dizzying relief swelled her chest, and she had to sit down on the porch steps. Rolfe sat beside her, his expression one of hope mingled with amusement.

"Oh, Rolfe!" She laughed, shaking her head. "I never expected such a sacrifice! I do love you so much!"

"That was all I wanted to hear," he said, his voice husky. He leaned forward almost tentatively and brushed his lips against hers. Milly quivered at the tenderness of his touch. How had she ever come to deserve a man such as this?

"I need you, too," Milly confessed against his lips. "I need you to be solid for me, to give my life structure and keep my feet on the ground. I think I've always been looking for you."

"Solid and dependable, that's me," Rolfe said with a grin. "I sound like an insurance company."

"For heart, home, and life," Milly said.

Rolfe's thumb rubbed the delicate bone in her jaw. "That sounded suspiciously like a proposal."

"Decent or indecent?" Milly asked coyly.

"Oh, decent, by all means," Rolfe growled, gathering her up high in his arms. "But not just at the moment."

"Rolfe!" Milly laughed and struggled half-heartedly as he mounted the steps and kicked open the door to the empty house. He paused midway through the small living room and glanced at her.

"We won't have to live here, you know," he said.

Milly's arms tightened around his neck. "I want to

live in your house," she said in a small voice. "I don't want money to make any difference."

"It won't, honey. I think we're intelligent enough to deal with our business obligations without it affecting our chosen life-style. We both know that monetary success isn't necessarily a measure of happiness. We can relax knowing that our family is comfortable, but I don't think we'll let it go to our heads. As long as we love each other, it can never be a threat again."

"Oh, Rolfe, do you really think so?" Milly asked hopefully, tightening her clasp about his neck. She felt a great weight lift from her at the confident assurance in Rolfe's voice.

"I know so. I love you for what you are, not for what you own. Everyone in town has already welcomed you into their hearts. You're sweet and funny and utterly lovable, and I intend to spend the rest of my life proving it to you. But that's not what I meant about the house. I bought you an early wedding present."

"Oh, really? Kind of cocky, aren't you?" She nuzzled his neck. She could feel his smile.

"I had high hopes. But don't you want to know what it is?"

"Hmmm?" Milly's lips were doing delightful things to Rolfe's neck. He groaned and began to move toward the bedroom.

"I said . . ."

"Later," she murmured, planting tiny feather kisses along his jawline. Her hands explored the purple fabric of his costume. "How do you get out of this thing, anyway?"

Rolfe's chuckle was throaty and seductive. "I thought you'd never ask."

Clothes and costumes were swiftly shed until they stood in each other's arms, hip pressed to hip, hands seeking as mouths joined in silent communion. Rolfe cupped the rounded globes of Milly's breasts, her skin pearly and luminous in the darkness of the room. His thumbs stroked the tips into hard nubs, and Milly moaned as her insides melted into liquid heat.

"Oh, God, Milly," Rolfe murmured. "Are you really here? Really mine?"

"Yes, oh yes! For always," Milly gasped. She clung to him, smoothing the hard muscle of his sinewy arms, exploring the trim line of waist and flanks. A sense of exultation filled Milly even as passion spiraled upward. They had passed their trial by fire and were together at last. Problems might still test their love, but they would face them side by side with tolerance and humor, their differences balancing them, their love sustaining them.

Rolfe lowered Milly onto the waiting bed, and their glances meshed. The starlight filtered in through the open window, touching Rolfe's face with silver and spangling the gilt of his hair. Milly touched his face, moved nearly to tears by the tenderness that lifted his lips and softened his eyes.

"Ah, love," he breathed, placing a kiss on her trembling lips. "You don't know what you do to me." His mouth moved lower, found the bud of her nipple and laved the silken flesh. The rough texture of his tongue was an intimate torture that made Milly writhe against him, seeking that other part of him that would make her whole.

"What? What do I do to you?" she moaned. Her hands threaded through the silky strands of his hair, pressing him closer.

"You make me burn with wanting you," Rolfe answered, his voice thick. Milly's fingers urgently traced the ridge of his spine down to his hips. The knowledge of his need for her fed her own desire, and her teeth nipped lightly at the velvet skin of his shoulder.

"Oh, Rolfe, I love you. I need you so much! Please . . ." Her request was stifled by Rolfe's lips on hers, then he lifted her hips and probed strongly against her. Milly arched against him as they became one and all thought ceased. There was only the fiery need, the conflagration of desire burning out of control in the beautiful act of love.

Rolfe's love made him gentle at first, but Milly's need drove him higher and higher until gentleness was forgotten in the boiling cauldron of mutual desire. When at last they reached the pinnacle, stars exploded behind Milly's eyes and she cried aloud as the ecstasy of fulfillment filled her being. Rolfe called her name, then he, too, joined her in the oblivion of completion.

They lay gasping for breath and Milly was not even aware of her tears until Rolfe's gentle kisses discovered them.

"You're crying! Oh, God, honey, did I hurt you?" he asked in horror. Milly shook her head, feeling utterly content.

"No, you didn't hurt me. You're so wonderful," she whispered. "I've never been so happy."

Rolfe relaxed at her words and cuddled her beside him. "It's only the beginning for us, honey," he said, his voice deep with emotion. "Now that I've got you, I'll never let you go."

"Good." Milly sighed and snuggled closer. Suddenly a thought struck her. She raised up on one elbow, and a slight frown creased her brow. "Rolfe, what about the ball? Do you think we should go back? They'll be looking for us."

"Don't be ridiculous," he replied easily. "Nobody in their right minds expects us to reappear."

"But what will people think?"

"I'm sure that we'll be forgiven, since I intend to make you Mrs. Rolfe Hart as soon as the law allows. Sooner, if it can be arranged. Will you wear that old-fashioned wedding dress you had on in the attic that day? I'll never forget how beautiful you looked."

"If you want," she promised, pleased and touched by his request.

"Oh, yes, I definitely want," he murmured huskily. "Unfortunately, I don't think I have the energy to do anything about it right now."

"And whose fault is that?" she asked impishly. She lay across his chest, resting her chin in her palms and gazing down adoringly into his deep blue eyes. Even in the darkness she could see their azure gleam, and she exulted in the relaxed and loving expression on his handsome face. His large hands caressed her spine, pausing to cup a saucy buttock.

"A sexy wench that's made me putty in her little hands," he murmured. His fingers slipped into her hair and pulled her lips down to his. Milly was breathing heavily when she raised her head.

"You, sir, have a one-track mind," she accused with a shaky laugh.

"Come back here, you," he ordered.

"Oh, no, not until you tell me about that wedding present you mentioned."

"Wondered when you'd come back to that," he said with a laugh, settling her more securely against him.

"Come on, give!" She ran a light finger down Rolfe's rib cage, and he squirmed under her delicate torture. He laughed and caught her hand, then pressed a sensuous kiss into her sensitive palm.

"I bought us the Abington house." His voice was muffled against her hand, and Milly shook her head as if she hadn't heard correctly.

"What?" Her voice was faint.

188

"I hope you'll approve. I couldn't let Dean Single-ton get his hands on it. The vineyards are worth saving, and I know how much you admire the old place, so I thought . . ."

She could feel his shrug. "But what about Florie and Louella?"

"It seems this crisis has been what they've been waiting for. After fifty years, Buford finally popped the question to Florie, and she's accepted."

"You mean they're getting married?" Milly gasped.

"Don't look so surprised," he laughed. "The best people do, you know."

"It's wonderful! But what about Louella? How can she leave her home?"

"She thinks it's a godsend. She's heard of a retirement village in Fayetteville close to the university. She plans to buy a condominium and work on her research. Of course, she might have tried to hold on to the house longer if Dean had been the only one interested. But she knows we'll appreciate its heritage."

"I can't believe it," Milly whispered, her throat tight with emotion.

"We could fix it up," Rolfe said diffidently. "You know about things like that. Of course, I want you to continue with your auctioneering for as long as you want. I just thought that house would make a good home for us. Those wide porches would be great for kids, but if you don't want to do that—" He broke off as Milly struggled with the lump in her throat. "I'm sorry, Milly. If you don't like that idea we'll do something else."

"Like it?" she croaked, then flung herself across his chest and began to kiss him feverishly. "It's what I've always dreamed of! Oh, Rolfe! You marvelous, crazy, solid and respectable man! How I love you!"

Rolfe, feeling disgustingly proud of himself, decided

189

to take advantage of the situation. A long while later, when their breathing had once again returned to normal, they lay satiated, touching and stroking idly in the aftermath of love.

"So you think that it's a good idea to fill up those porches with a big family?" Rolfe asked languidly.

"Marvelous idea," Milly agreed.

"I can see it now. Scores of young'uns playing chase all over the house, each dressed in tiny purple tights!" Rolfe's voice was filled with suppressed laughter.

"Oh, no! You'll never live down your reputation as the Purple Avenger as it is!" Milly protested. "I won't have my children dressed as miniature versions!"

"I thought you liked the Purple Avenger," Rolfe said, acting a bit hurt. "Why, I planned to repeat my role every year!"

"Oh, God!" Milly shuddered at the thought. "Rolfe, I'll marry you, but only if you'll promise me one thing."

"What, love?" Rolfe murmured, his gaze adoring.

"Promise me you'll never, *ever* wear purple tights again!"

Catch up with any ♡ ♡ Candlelights you're missing.

Here are the Ecstasies published this past August

ECSTASY SUPREMES $2.75 each

- ☐ 133 SUSPICION AND DESIRE, JoAnna Brandon . 18463-0-11
- ☐ 134 UNDER THE SIGN OF SCORPIO, Pat West . . 19158-0-27
- ☐ 135 SURRENDER TO A STRANGER, Dallas Hamlin 18421-5-12
- ☐ 136 TENDER BETRAYER, Terri Herrington 18557-2-18

ECSTASY ROMANCES $2.25 each

- ☐ 450 SWEET REVENGE, Tate McKenna 18431-2-10
- ☐ 451 FLIGHT OF FANCY, Jane Atkin 12649-5-11
- ☐ 452 THE MAVERICK AND THE LADY,
  Heather Graham 15207-0-34
- ☐ 453 NO GREATER LOVE, Jan Stuart 16377-3-28
- ☐ 454 THE PERFECT MATCH, Anna Hudson 16947-X-37
- ☐ 455 STOLEN PASSION, Alexis Hill Jordan 18394-4-23

- ☐ 1 *THE TAWNY GOLD MAN*, Amii Lorin 18978-0-35
- ☐ 2 *GENTLE PIRATE*, Jayne Castle 12981-8-33

At your local bookstore or use this handy coupon for ordering:

Dell DELL READERS SERVICE—DEPT. B1271A
P.O. BOX 1000, PINE BROOK, N.J. 07058

Please send me the above title(s). I am enclosing $_____$ (please add 75¢ per copy to cover postage and handling). Send check or money order—no cash or CODs. Send check or money order—no cash or CODs. Please allow 3-4 weeks for shipment.
<u>CANADIAN ORDERS: please submit in U.S. dollars.</u>

Ms./Mrs./Mr._____

Address_____

City/State_____ Zip_____